She loved him, she really did, but he was asking for something she just couldn't do…

Mara and Adrian drove to the water's edge to watch the sunset. After the surfers deserted the beach, Adrian stood up, peeled off his clothes, and held his hand out to her. "We swim."

The sky was dotted with hundreds of stars. He smiled at her and yanked her T-shirt over her head.

Mara's throat closed up. "I can't." She could barely speak. "I don't swim. I'm afraid of the water. I don't go into the waves, Adrian, ever."

"I will show you," he said. "You will be safe."

Fighting panic, she held onto his broad shoulders as he drew her to her feet then tugged down her shorts and panties before rolling their clothes up in a towel.

She ran her hand down his smooth, hard chest, before going lower to the loincloth he still wore.

He caught her hand and brought it to his lips, pressing his lips to her palm. "We swim now," he said and led her to the water.

She stuck her toe in, and a smothering panic settled like a stone on her chest, making it impossible to breathe. Desperate, she ran back toward the towel. "I can't."

"Yes, darling, you can," he said.

She shook her head violently and wept. "I can't, Adrian. I'm sorry."

He's waited for her for centuries, and now it's almost too late…

Adrian, a merman and heir to the throne of Crystal City, lives deep under the ocean riptides. He's waited a lifetime for Mara, his destined mate, and now time is running out. She must come willingly with him to the city before the deadline or he forfeits his right to rule. The only problem? Mara thinks she's human and is deathly afraid of the water.

She belongs with him, but he's asking more than she can give…

Mara has had an unreasonable fear of water for as long as she can remember. Thinking herself a simple kindergarten teacher from Michigan, she believes the mystery man she makes love to when she sleeps is only a figment of her lonely imagination. On vacation in Hawaii, Mara is thrilled to discover her dream lover is real flesh and blood—until he asks her to forsake everything she knows and follow him under the riptides, the very last place she wants to go.

KUDOS for *Under the Riptides*

In *Under the Riptides* by Tara Eldana, Mara believes she is just a simple kindergarten teacher. She doesn't know she's special in any way. But Adrian does. He's a merman and Mara is his destined mate. When she goes to Hawaii for her summer vacation from school in Michigan, Adrian is ecstatic, but Mara thinks he's just a dream, as she has only seen him when she's sleeping. Then Adrian shows up when she's at the beach and wide awake and Mara doesn't know what to think. But when he asks her to follow him home, Mara is devastated. She can't go in the water. She's terrified of it. Like Eldana's last book, this steamy romance is hot. It's got a clever and unique plot, lots of spicy lovemaking, and endearing characters that you can't help rooting for. ~ *Taylor Jones, Reviewer*

Under the Riptides is another steamy romance from Tara Eldana. Unlike her first book, however, this one is a paranormal romance, with an unusual twist. The book's about shifters, as most paranormal romances are, but this one's about merpeople. Adrian, a merman, has been waiting for Mara for a long time. Now she's finally here, but there's a problem. Mara doesn't believe Adrian's anything more than a dream. Even when he shows up in the daytime and shows her that she is a shifter like he is, she has a hard time believing him. And when he asks her to leave her brother and dementia-afflicted mother and follow him beneath the waves, she's horrified. With a pathological fear of water and drowning, going into the ocean *not* Mara's idea of a good time. But if she doesn't follow Adrian home willingly, he will lose the right to rule his kingdom. Kind of a no-win situation for everybody. I think Eldana did an excellent job of showing us the almost insurmountable obstacles standing between the two would-be mates, such as a language barrier, the whole paranormal belief thing since Mara thinks she's human, as well as the fact that she's terrified of water. The author handled it all with sensitivity and charisma, and let's not forget the hot sex scenes. ~ Regan Murphy, Reviewer

ACKNOWLEDGEMENTS

To the dream team at Black Opal Books, Lauri Wellington, for giving me a chance to tell my stories and editors Shannon and fabulous Faith for making them the best they could be.

To Julie Stevens (Photography by Julie) for playing mermaid and taking the perfect photo for the cover.

To my husband, children, sisters, parents and friends for their support and the fabulous professionals at St. John Providence Hospital in Southfield, Michigan who gave me my life back.

To the writing community at Black Opal Books and the members of the Greater Detroit Romance Writers of America for their invaluable support and encouragement.

Under
The
RIPTIDES

Tara Eldana

A Black Opal Books Publication

DEDICATION

Chapter 1

Mara entered the last grade into her laptop for the report cards that would be issued to her kindergarten students later that week, still smarting from the "needs improvement" evaluation her principal gave her.

As much as she loved her students, her heart wasn't in teaching. In fact, it wasn't in anything, except leaving Grand Rapids, Michigan, even if it was for only the summer. She checked her travel plans for the bazilliointh time, excitement bubbling in her veins. Her friend Kristen couldn't believe Mara had found such a great deal on a

Hawaiian timeshare for the entire summer. Granted, the condo was tiny and located in a secluded part of Kauai, known as the garden island. Even though there was not a lot of nightlife, it sounded like heaven to Mara.

She checked her cell phone and saw two missed calls from her mother. "Crap." Taking several deep breaths, she dialed. She so hated to miss her mother's calls. Alice suffered from fast-onset Alzheimer's and only phoned when she had a good day and remembered who Mara was.

Hoping her mother was lucid, Mara decided to stop at the assisted living center. When she got there, her mother had lost her thread of memory.

"I'll be gone for a while, Mom, to Hawaii."

"You're so pretty. What is your name?"

"It's Mara, Mom. Gary thinks I'm nuts to go there, because I can't swim."

"I used to swim with someone. His name was Gary, too."

"That was Dad, Mom, he was a doctor. And Gary is your son. He's a doctor like dad was."

Her mother got agitated. Mara called for the nurses and kissed her mother's forehead, sighing.

Her father had died two years ago of a sudden heart attack and she and Gary watched over their mother.

Gary and his wife Jana urged Mara take a vacation, although they were amazed she chose Hawaii because she'd never learned to swim. They lived in Michigan, surrounded by water, and swimming terrified her. But she was determined to change from the dowdy, drab, aimless, scared twenty-five-year-old she had somehow morphed into. And something inside her was urging her to take this trip.

That night, Mara held the quartz crystal her father had given her in her palm as she stretched out in her bed and tried to relax. He gave it to her and said it was the same color as water, but it didn't move so she didn't have to be scared of it. Other than Kristen, her mother, and brother, Mara had no one to hold her here. Besides her chances of getting tenure at her school weren't looking good after her "needs improvement" review. She sighed at her bleak thoughts, tightened her hold on the crystal, and closed her eyes to sleep. She had an early flight to catch.

ⒺⓈⒺⓈ

Mara nearly took a header as she dragged her bags up the steps to the timeshare. It had rained an hour ago, but the ground was still a bit muddy. She slipped the flats she traveled in off and took care with her suitcases so she wouldn't track any mud indoors.

Mara couldn't put a name to the flower-adorned bushes surrounding the tiny cottage billed as an artist's or writer's retreat, but their sweet subtle fragrance filled the rooms. The bedroom was barely large enough to hold a full-sized bed and small closet. The living room had room for one white, oversized sofa and a flat-screen TV. Even the kitchen was small, but serviceable with a tiny table fit for two.

She should unpack then see about groceries, but she was exhausted. She stretched out on the bed, breathed in the salt air and flowers, clutched the quartz crystal she'd brought with her, and shut her eyes…

ℰↄℰↄ

She stood in a great hall under the sea, with marble columns and crystal pillars, wearing a long, snowy white robe with a silken sash. Water flowed in channels at the edges of the room. The surrounding crystal reflected the ruby necklace encircling her throat.

He stood next to her, clasping her left hand. His sandy brown hair, streaked with gold, reached his shoulders.

They were both barefoot, facing an altar of white marble.

Others, wearing robes, watched them.

The man squeezed her hand, smiled into her eyes, and took hold of her other hand, linking them. Another man read from a scroll he held. She couldn't understand the words until he said, "Mara and Adrian."

The man, who must have been Adrian, stepped closer, took hold of her waist, and squeezed her left hand. She smiled into his questioning eyes and nodded. Pleasure lit his face. The crowd murmured and Adrian touched his forehead to hers.

The man by the altar continued and, when he fell silent, the crowd cheered. Many smiled at them. Some clapped. Adrian led her to a crystal pyramid as the onlookers tossed blossoms of water lilies at their feet. A bright pink bloom fell on Mara's hair. Adrian tucked it behind her left ear and winked.

He reclaimed her waist as they glided underwater through passageways. Oddly, she wasn't afraid of being underwater, nor did she have to hold her breath. They came to a chamber and she stepped out of the water while he kept firm hold on her.

Adrian shrugged out of his robe. Now naked save for his loincloth, he strode to a table and rearranged the large crystals decorating its top. Lean and muscled, he moved with fluid grace.

The room wavered and changed and a bed appeared. Mara moved toward it. She brushed her hand over the fabric, amazed at how soft and light it felt. Adrian watched her, a question in his eyes.

ᘓᘓᘓ

Mara's eyes flew open. Her heart thumped hard in chest, as if she'd been running, not sleeping. She shook off the images of her crazy, jet-lagged dream and put on her shoes. Then she grabbed her purse and digital camera. She needed some fresh island air, sun, and sand to clear the crazy dreams out of her head. The island beckoned. She didn't come all this way to sleep. Maybe the drive to Hanalei, where they'd shot scenes for the movie *South Pacific* would be a good change of scenery and an escape from the weirdness in her head. It wasn't too far, and she could stop for groceries on her way back.

Her hand strayed to her throat. It felt bare without the ruby necklace she'd worn in her dream.

Seated in her rented Corolla, she started the engine fiddled with the radio. The Everly Brothers sang, "All I Have to do is Dream."

"Perfect," she said, switching it off. She pulled over into a scenic overlook and parked behind a couple of other cars. Far below, surfers were riding the waves. She looked through the camera's viewfinder and pushed the zoom lens.

One of the surfers walked out of the shallows. His wet hair hung to his shoulders. Prickles of awareness rose on the back of Mara's neck and her heart pounded. She zoomed closer. He looked in her direction, then stopped mid-stride, as if he could see her.

Fighting the urge to run to him, she rubbed her suddenly throbbing temples. Her heart raced. He looked just like the man in her dream. This was nuts, right? Was she losing her grip on reality? Maybe it was the jet-lag? Either way, her legs went weak and she dropped like a sopping wet towel on to a bench, dragging in deep breaths. Minutes ticked by, but she finally got her heart rate under control.

"Are you okay?"

Mara looked up into a pair of kind blue eyes. The man was about her brother's age with short brown hair and a friendly smile.

"Jet-lag," Mara said, standing up.

He pushed her gently back down on the bench and sat next to her. "Take a minute."

"I need to get some groceries," she said, stifling a yawn. "Is there someplace close?"

He nodded. "Not too far. Turn left when you pull out. I'm Mike. I write for the local newspaper."

He took her hand and helped her to her feet. His fingers felt warm and strong.

"I'm Mara. I teach kindergarten in Michigan. At least, I did last week."

Mike chuckled. "Your name, it means 'the sea.'" His gaze went to the surfers.

"Thanks." Mara forced herself to look toward the beach. Her surfer was gone. Her heart sank. "I should get going." She began to walk to her car.

Mike fell into step beside her and smiled. "Lettuce costs a fortune," he warned. "The tourists are always surprised."

"Thanks again," she said.

He handed her his business card. "Call or text if you

want to know where anything else is. My cell is on there." He smiled, again.

She smiled back, gave him a little wave, and thought, *Okay, he's interested.*

He walked to his car, a Corolla, identical to her rental. "Nice to meet you."

She laughed and tucked his business card into her purse. Fighting exhaustion, she picked up some groceries and headed home. After stashing them in the fridge, she laid down on the couch, this time hoping for dreamless, or least sane, sleep.

∽∾∽∾

Adrian stood absolutely still. Mara stepped forward and cradled his face in an effort to soothe him. He shut his eyes and sighed, then pressed his warm mouth to her palm.

"Mara." He said her name with tenderness, even while his gaze raked over her possessively. He put his hands on her waist and drew her closer, enveloping her in his scent of musk and rain. Unfastening her gold sash, he pressed his lips to the curve of her neck. She sighed, longing to be free of her gown. Adrian's hands adjusted something near the small of her back and the gown fell away, to puddle at her feet, leaving her naked.

He cupped her breasts and teased her nipples into tight, pink pebbles. He smiled into her eyes and then lifted her into his arms. After gently placing her on the bed, he tugged on the necklace. Fierce possession lit his eyes with golden lights.

"Mine." His hand brushed against her jaw, drifted over her bare shoulder, feathered down her ribs over her stomach, before moving lower still. She bucked against him.

He stared into her eyes, his lips inches from hers. "Mine, Mara." He touched her core, and she jerked. "You must say it," he growled.

She nodded. "Yes, yours." She swallowed hard.

"Only mine," he breathed into her mouth.

"Only yours," she said.

He kissed her then.

Chapter 2

Adrian stood before the Council, silently cursing them for summoning him so suddenly as he listened to Lorion drone on and on. He'd been watching Mara, albeit at a distance, but he couldn't ignore a Council summons, not until he assumed his duties as ruler.

"Your time is running out. We need a ruler to represent us in the summit of the Crystal Cities," Lorion said.

"That is not until the fat moon in August." Adrian kept his voice calm. It wouldn't do to anger the old windbag.

Besides, Lorion's status as an Elder deserved respect,

especially since he'd inhabited these depths for some thousand years.

"But you only have until then to walk on land. And she is spending time with the human man, the scribe," Lorion argued, narrowing his eyes.

Adrian's life force ran hot. His aunt Nitia, newly appointed to the Council, patted his shoulder to calm him. When the scribe dared to put his hands on Mara, Adrian had nearly snatched her away. Unfortunately, such actions required him to warp space to get to her, which would risk discovery by the humans.

"She saw the scribe once, briefly." Adrian made a supreme effort to unclench his jaw. He had to get through this and onto the island where Mara waited.

"If she does not accept you—"

Adrian cut Lorion off. "She already has."

Lorion narrowed his eyes again. "How so?"

"After we were joined in the Great Hall." He did not add "marriage bed," but it was understood. He wouldn't speak of joining with her while she slept in her human form.

Lorion waved his hand in dismissal.

"This Mara, she believes you are a dream, nothing more. And she is afraid of water. She does not swim."

"She is frightened," Adrian said. "I will teach her and make her understand."

The other Council members murmured their assent.

Lorion shook his head. "You have convinced the majority, just as your mother did, hence their consensus."

Adrian's fingers balled into fists at the mention of his mother.

"You are determined as she was," Lorion continued. "I have grave doubts you will get the outcome you seek. You are as unwilling as she to listen to me."

The Council bent their heads in honor of Lisia and Anapa's memory. Adrian's parents were killed by human weaponry. His father, Anapa, had insisted on returning to Tahiti to warn his people of the human submarines armed with torpedoes hunting in the waters. They had left Adrian in the care of his Aunt Nitia, safe in the depths of the ocean. One of those torpedoes killed Lisia and Anapa as they headed back to the Crystal City, leaving Adrian an orphan.

Adrian did not lift his face until all the Council members had done so.

"Leave us," Nitia said to Adrian.

The Council chanted words of protection for Adrian. He expressed his thanks and breathed into his sea form.

☙❧☙

Mara sat on a bench at Waimea Canyon with her camera in her lap and committed the beautiful panoramic view to memory, since capturing it on film was an impossibility. A man with tanned, leathery skin sat in front of his easel and canvas, mixing paint colors on his palette.

The sun sparkled across the turquoise waves and the scent of the coconut oil she'd rubbed into her skin wafted in the gentle breeze.

She had phoned her mother, emailed Kristen and her brother. The call with her mother hadn't gone well, and Mara ended the call before her mother grew agitated.

Mara had tentative plans to eat dinner with Mike. He said he would text her if his editor wanted him to cover a community town hall meeting tonight. She hoped he could make it. But she doubted there would be anything but friendship between them.

Whoosh. The hairs on the back of her neck stood up as a flash of white passed overhead.

"A white owl," the artist said.

"What?" she asked. She'd been afraid to speak for fear of disturbing his artistic flow.

"That was a white owl," he said. "Here in the islands, it means changes, big time." He returned to his work.

"Oh, thanks." She stood and began walking toward her car. Prickles of awareness tingled through her veins as she realized a man stood near her car.

Drawing closer, she realized it was him, the man from her dreams.

She stumbled and he was at her side, his hands circling her waist. She leaned into his strength and his familiar scent of musk and rain wrapped around her.

Dreams didn't come with smells, did they? How could she be asleep?

She stepped back and took deep breaths. He was a head taller than her, dressed in cargo shorts and an olive T-shirt that stretched over his broad shoulders and leanly muscled arms. Just like her dream lover. So maybe his stomach and butt were as ripped and tight as her imaginary lover, too?

He tucked a strand of her hair behind her ear. "You are not dreaming."

"Yes, I am." She shook her head, then in her best no-nonsense teacher's voice chided, "And now I'm talking to myself."

"No, Mara."

Panic seized her. This figment of her imagination knew her name. He still held her around her waist, which was good since her knees had turned to jelly.

The artist had gathered his things and was walking toward his car. "You two all right?" he called.

"Yes," the man holding her said.

"He can see you?" Her voice sounded hysterical.

In answer, he covered her lips with his, silencing her. He tasted the same as she dreamed. Her mind spun, cascading over the impossibility of a dream becoming reality. Well, at least she wasn't in front of a room of kindergartners kissing a figment of her imagination.

He lifted his head, and she stared into the same sea-green eyes as her yummy dream guy. She sighed. Thank God she still had her health insurance, because therapy bills were going to be out of this world. Still, she would miss him when she was cured of whatever this was.

Distantly, she was aware of the artist's chuckle and then the slam of a car door.

She pulled back from Adrian as the car pulled away. She stumbled toward her own car, half expecting him to be gone when she looked up.

He wasn't. He stood there, staring at her neck, then reached into a pocket and pulled out a necklace of brilliant red stones. Those couldn't be real rubies, they were too huge.

He came toward her, his gaze questioning.

She stood, stupidly gaping at him.

He lifted her hair and fastened the necklace at her nape. The sun caught the stones and they glittered like fire. He laughed with joy, pulled her back against his chest, and trailed kisses to her ear.

Her traitorous nipples grew taut and her body melted into him. "No." She stepped away from him. She needed answers "This…you…we don't make sense," she said.

He stared down at the car, then up at the gathering clouds. It would rain soon.

"Take us to where you sleep and I will tell you," he said.

She shook with nerves. Who was he? Would she be safe with him?

"Mara." He gently took hold of her hand and then lifted it to his lips, pressing a kiss into her palm. Electricity shot up her arm.

"I don't know your name," she whispered.

He pulled her into his arms again and pressed a kiss to her forehead. "You do." He murmured something in a language she couldn't understand then moved his lips to her ear. "I am called Adrian. You may also say…" He whispered a strange word.

She shook her head. "I don't understand." She wondered if anyone would spare them a second glance. Did they look like a couple on their honeymoon?

He lifted her chin, and his lips brushed over hers. Her lips parted, giving him full access, and her body melted once more into his arms. This was madness, pure and simple. He broke off the kiss with obvious reluctance and then cradled her head against his chest until her lips were nestled in the base of his throat

"I am 'Adrian' as you are…" He said the strange word again. "Others call me, Lord Adrian." He pressed her closer. "You may also say husband."

"Husband?"

He let her go and looked toward the sky. "We go before the water comes." It wasn't a question.

Mara opened the car door and slid behind the wheel. Adrian tried to open the passenger door, but it was locked. She slid across the seat and unlocked and opened it. He sat and slammed the door so hard the window rattled. She drove back to her condo.

Chapter 3

The rain came as Mara opened the door. Adrian stood next to her, taking deep breaths. So, like Mara, he liked the smell of rain. The acrid bite of ozone called to part of her soul.

She made her way through the tiny space and sank down onto the oversize couch. She fingered the necklace and stared at his broad shoulders as he studied her temporary home. The same necklace she'd seen in the dream, when she stood in the hall filled with crystal. But that was a dream, nothing else, surely.

He came to her side and took her in his arms.

She stared into his eyes. She felt dizzy with the

thoughts screaming in her head. "You said husband. That I could call you husband."

His smile was tender, and he nodded.

"You said 'mine' in our chamber, but I was asleep. It wasn't real." She touched the necklace, her words sounding weak even to her.

He kissed her.

She sighed into his mouth and then pulled away. He growled his disapproval. But this wasn't getting her anywhere. She wanted answers.

His green eyes danced with mischief. "Mara." He said her name like a phrase in a song. "No dream." He stared at her intently. "I wait for you." He seemed to search for a word. "So long, I wait for you." He caressed her neck and then cupped the necklace. The stones sparkled with a life of their own.

Before she knew his intention, he pulled her T-shirt over her head. Stunned, she moved to cover her bare breasts. With no kids or boss to see her, she hadn't bothered with a bra. Stunned, she felt the heat fill her face, but he wasn't looking at her breasts. Her hands fell to her hip bones. She wanted this—wanted him.

He lifted her auburn tresses off her shoulders and wrapped them around his hand. He massaged first one shoulder, then the other. The tension, she didn't realize she carried, dissolved. He settled the necklace so it lay across the top curves of her breasts.

When he cupped her breasts in his palms, she

gasped. Her nipples instantly hardened. He chuckled and pinched them. Pleasure shot to her core. His voice rumbled in approval and his face darkened with pleasure. Arching her back, she realized she liked to please him.

"Mine, Mara." He pressed his mouth to hers with fierce tenderness then lifted her in his arms. "Bathroom?" He seemed to choose the word with great thought.

She pointed and he strode into her tiny bathroom. After removing her panties and shorts, he put her in the bathtub and turned on the faucet, his green eyes lit with mischief. What was he doing? More importantly, why was she letting him?

As if reading her mind, he said, "You see." As water filled the tub, he sang words she didn't understand. She closed her eyes and stretched out. He sang with ease and sounded amazing. His voice as good, or better, than any lead vocalist she could think of.

When the water lapped her shoulders, he turned off the faucet. Through her lashes she watched him soap up his hands then glide them over every inch of her. He pressed between her legs and she opened for him, caught in a strange spell of need.

He had a thing for water. And she was sick of being scared of it. She never lingered in the shower. But what could happen in a bath tub? If things got too weird, she would just get out.

He pressed his fingers to her core and brought her quickly to a screaming climax. His hand cupped her chin and he lowered his lips to hers. Helpless to resist him, she sighed into his mouth, and put her arms around his neck to pull him closer. He deepened the kiss and she felt a tingling in her feet that travelled up her legs, only to stop at her waist.

It was not unpleasant or painful, just odd.

Mara broke off the kiss. Adrian took hold of her waist and she blinked in wonder.

A tail, she had a tail.

In vivid hues of sunset orange and sky blue, it was like gossamer. She lifted it out of the water. The same colors seeped up to her waist. Her legs had disappeared. She was fish from the waist down.

"Holy hell," she breathed, since she didn't have to watch her language in front of kindergartners.

Adrian looked at her tenderly. "We are the same."

Shouldn't she be hysterical or screaming in terror by now? What had this man done to her? And why had she let him? Who and what was he, really? Did it matter? This felt so right in every cell of her being and it was flat out impossible.

"Adrian." His name left her lips like a caress.

He lifted her out of the water and carried her to the couch. As she lay on the cushions he caressed her shoulders, her breasts, and moved down to where the juncture of her thighs had been. The tingling returned.

"Mara." He said more words she didn't understand, but she could see he was utterly pleased, which thrilled her. The tingling traveled from her waist to the end of her beautiful tail, and then it was gone, leaving her to stare at her boring feet and legs.

She put her arms around his neck. "Do it again, darling, please?"

∾◌∾

"Darling?" Adrian repeated. Did that mean Mara loved him?

He cursed his laziness during his language classes. He understood her English much better than he could speak it. He'd have to remedy that. Perhaps if they watched her television?

"Not now, darling," he said. He stood up and held his hand out. "Bed, where you sleep?"

She placed her hands in his and rose. She glanced down at her feet, her face soft with amazement, before she led him to where she slept. Water from the clouds pattered on the roof. Standing before her bed, she bit her lip. There was so much to tell her, but not now. He pulled his T-shirt over his head and stepped out of his shorts, leaving on his loincloth.

She watched him from under her lashes. When his sweet, shy, delicious wife demanded answers in her stern teacher's voice, he would give them to her, as he would give her his world and her destiny.

He stretched out in her bed, inhaling her scent on the

linen, and patted the space next to him. "Come here, by me. We talk."

She came. "Talk?" She sounded disappointed.

Seeing the quartz crystal she kept by her bedside, he reached over and picked it up. Holding it so it would catch the light, he invoked Sedna, She Who Watched Over the Waves, then set it on Mara's forehead, above the bridge of her nose. He waited as what she thought were her dreams, all of them, played back for them both—their first joining, the nights she'd spent in his arms, the ceremony in the Crystal City when he became her husband, and her pledge to him in their bedchamber that she was unequivocally his. At the end, she gave a delicate shiver that had him chuckling.

"Enough," he said, setting the quartz crystal back on her nightstand.

She caressed his jaw then explored the ridge of his shoulders, before drifting her hands down across his chest. Now, it was his turn to shiver.

"This seems so real." She lifted on one elbow to look at him. Joy danced in her blue eyes, changing the color to aquamarine then back to cloudy blue. "Why me, Adrian?"

He loved hearing his name on her lips. He raised an eyebrow in question.

"My mother—she isn't in her right mind and, even if she was, how could I ever explain this—us—to her, or my brother? How is this happening? Or am I losing my mind like she did? I'm just a kindergarten teacher without tenure."

He held her beautiful face in his hands. "You are…you will be…lady when I take you home."

She laid her head on his chest. "Where is home?" she said.

"Home in water, under water," he said.

She lifted her head. "So, you're a—"

He lifted strands of her hair from her face. "The same as I showed you before."

She shook her head, confusion clouding her pretty face. Her hand trailed down his chest, toward his loin-cloth. His hardness longed for her touch.

"But if we both have…" She swallowed hard.

"Sea forms?" he offered.

She nodded. "Yes, sea forms, how do we…" Her cheeks flamed red.

He rolled her underneath him, his erection pressing into the juncture of her thighs. She arched against him.

"Do what, darling?" Every time he called her darling, her eyes turned the color of waves.

"This," she whispered. "How do we do this when we have sea forms?"

He caressed her breasts, teasing her nipples into tight pink pebbles.

"I can't think when you do that." Her hands fumbled, trying to remove his loincloth.

"We are like this to join." He pressed a kiss to her

forehead, where he'd placed the quartz crystal. "Like you remember in our chamber at home."

"Oh," she said.

He suckled on her nipples and she writhed underneath him. He parted her legs. "I must make you remember."

"Darling," she gasped, looking down at their bodies pressed together. When she raised her head to meet his gaze, her blue eyes were a stormy gray. "I'm not, I don't use birth control."

"Birth control?" he asked. What did she mean? Damn her English words.

Color rose along her cheeks. She bit her lip. "I don't have any condoms." She looked so sweet and determined as she licked her lips nervously. The small movement made him harder. "Babies, Adrian. I want them, but not yet."

Finally understanding, he let out the breath he'd been holding and licked the valley of her breasts. He laid his hand on her soft, flat stomach. Would he ever grow tired of looking at her? "Not here. It cannot happen here, only at home." He stared into her ever-changing eyes, which were now light as the sky. "Not..." He searched for the right words. "Not possible here, only under the waves." He positioned himself at the juncture of her thighs and gazed at her in silent question.

"Please, Adrian," she said, moving against him.

He chuckled. He knew that word. Please her he

would. He licked her stiff nipples then moved lower to where soft curls covered her core. Her legs fell open and she clutched handfuls of his hair as he took his time teasing her with his tongue, until she was moaning his name. Using his mouth and fingers, he sent her over the edge.

Unable to wait any longer to be inside her, he thrust into her hard, filling and stretching her. Careful to stay buried deep inside her, he rolled so she was astride him. At first, she was hesitant, but when she found her rhythm, she sent them both over the edge, screaming their love for each other.

They stayed locked together as they both drifted to sleep.

��

Adrian opened his eyes as Mara eased away from him. As she met his gaze, her skin glowed like moonlight.

She caressed his shoulder. "Bathroom. I need a shower."

He let her pull away but rolled out of the bed before she could stand. He gathered her in his arms and carried her the few steps. He pulled down the shower nozzle and turned on the faucet. He took her hand and stepped into the small space.

She watched him. "Adrian," she said, then licked her lips.

"Mara, what is wrong?"

"The water, if we do this together, will I…will you…"

"Change to sea form?"

"You know what I'm thinking?" she asked.

He pulled her close and kissed her till she was out of breath. Then he let her go. "Only if I wish it, when we are here. In the sea, it is different."

"Oh," she said. "If you swim in the ocean you change, but I wouldn't? Not automatically?"

He frowned. "Automatically?"

"Right away, as soon as I got wet," she explained.

He grinned and dipped his finger into her moist cleft. "Wet?"

She wouldn't look at him. "Yes," she answered softly. "Like that."

He pulled her into his arms. "If you wish it darling, you could change under the sea. Then we would have babies. Or you can stay as you are, and take sea form when I wish you to."

He set her away from him then lifted the necklace she'd worn since he first fastened it around her neck. He kept his voice calm, with no trace of mischief or a smile. "That way, no babies," he said. "You have free will."

"But we'd be like this?" She wrapped her hand around his erect cock and he groaned her name. "At your home, like in my dreams?"

He touched his forehead to hers, breathing hard. "No

dream, Mara, mine." He took hold of her necklace. "Yes, we are like this."

She put his hardness to her cleft and moaned. He lifted her until she could wrap her legs around his waist. She giggled and put her arms around his neck.

She smiled and his heart felt like it would explode. He would do anything, he realized, to see her smile at him like that.

Chapter 4

Mara and Adrian drove to the water's edge to watch the sunset. After the surfers deserted the beach, Adrian stood up, peeled off his clothes, and held his hand out to her. "We swim."

The sky was dotted with hundreds of stars. He smiled at her and yanked her T-shirt over her head.

Mara's throat closed up. "I can't." She could barely speak. "I don't swim. I'm afraid of the water. I don't go into the waves, Adrian, ever."

"I will show you," he said. "You will be safe."

Fighting panic, she held onto his broad shoulders as he drew her to her feet then tugged down her shorts and panties before rolling their clothes up in a towel. Her hands went to the necklace but she couldn't find the clasp.

He shook his head. "You wear it always."

"But what about the salt water?"

His hand rested on the curve of her throat. "Always, Mara." His voice held a steely resolve she never heard before.

She ran her hand down his smooth, hard chest, before going lower to the loincloth he still wore.

He caught her hand and brought it to his lips, pressing his lips to her palm. "We swim now," he said and led her to the water.

She stuck her toe in, and a smothering panic settled like a stone on her chest, making it impossible to breathe. Desperate, she ran back toward the towel. "I can't."

"Yes, darling, you can," he said.

She shook her head violently and wept. "I can't, Adrian. I'm sorry."

"Mara, you have beautiful sea form. You will have it again."

"But that was in the bathtub. I couldn't drown there."

"Drown?" he said.

"Perish, die," she sobbed.

"You will be in sea form, and I will keep you safe, always, in my arms."

She swallowed hard. Her tears ran down her face. The wetness tasted salty like the ocean that went on forever and would swallow her up. She'd bob in the waves like flotsam before she sank to oblivion.

"I wish it, Mara." The commanding tone was back.

"Are we going to your home?"

He nodded.

She couldn't just leave. Her brother was expecting her call tomorrow. If she didn't call, he would worry. Plus, she wanted to call her mother today. If she didn't, her mother would forget who Mara was to her. Then there was Mike, they were going to meet for lunch tomorrow.

Her mind reeled with every argument possible to stop her from doing something so flat out crazy. The times she'd spent in his arms were heaven. But was she ready to make it forever? "Will we come back here?"

He looked sad. He clenched his jaw and swallowed hard. "Yes, if you wish."

He sang her name melodically over and over, until the tension seeped from her body. Then he lifted her into his arms and stepped through the shallows. He kissed her before a wave engulfed them.

Her chest seized up and she felt faint. Was drowning painful? He kept firm hold of her as the tingling in her feet glided up to her waist. She studied him, his sea form resplendent in bold reds and blue under the moon and starlight. He was magnificent. Wanting to be with him, she dragged as much air into her lungs as she could, only to realize she was breathing under water.

He took hold of her waist as they swam, holding her close. He dipped his head to fuse her mouth with his until she felt winded. They rode a riptide that plunged them fathoms deep.

Here, the sea was dark and murky, but he moved fearlessly, keeping firm hold of Mara's waist as she grew more and more afraid in the swirling darkness. He squeezed her close in reassurance, but she was beyond panic. Finally, she saw lighted towers in the distance.

The image plunged her dreamlike fantasies into a re-alistic nightmare. A little hysterically, she wondered when she would wake up in her bed in Michigan, alone, with lessons to plan and a mother to care for.

They came to a circular structure made of white marble. Carved steps led to an entrance. On the step above the water, he settled her onto his lap. Maybe she was ill, or more likely, delirious because this couldn't possibly be real. Yet the feel of Adrian's hand as he stroked her back and shoulders until their sea forms sub-sided, was very real. He set her on her feet, which now seemed larger and wider than normal.

She stood on shaky legs, naked save her necklace sparkling like fire. Next to her, he stood naked as well, nothing but smooth skin, and lean muscles. Mesmerized, she couldn't take her eyes off him as he guided her to a chamber.

Inside, white robes and gold sashes from her dream were arranged on a marble table. Adrian put his garment on, tied the sash, and then dressed her. He tied the sash around her waist then traced her lips with his tongue. She opened her lips, drew his tongue inside, and then sucked on it. He moaned and pulled her hard against him.

He broke off the kiss and smiled into her eyes, his own lit with the gold she'd come to expect when he was pleased or about to instigate mischief.

Two women entered the chamber unannounced, dressed in blue gowns with their long, reddish-blonde hair artfully arranged with wreathes of flowers. Their un-lined faces, with high elegant cheekbones, made it diffi-cult to guess their ages. Their eyes were light hazel, and they looked like sisters.

Adrian squeezed her waist. "I leave now."

"No." Mara's voice rose, her panic back in full force.

He sang her name and touched his forehead to hers. Strangely, her panic evaporated.

The women murmured approvingly to each other.

"I see you soon, darling," he said then he kissed her.

She opened her lips and tasted him deeply. He lifted his mouth and stared into her eyes, a delicate tenderness reflected in his gaze.

She straightened her spine and smiled. He squeezed her waist and left.

The women gave her shy smiles then moved the quartz crystals on the table. Another chamber opened within the room. The walls sparkled with pink, perhaps rose quartz?

They motioned for her to sit on a cushioned chair. Mara cautiously took a seat, and they began to arrange her hair into an elaborate updo, weaving jewels into the strands. They moved the crystals again, and a white light filled the chamber for an instant. Her wet hair was now dry. They smoothed a rose scented lotion on her hands, feet, arms, and shoulders. From some sort of artist's palette, they applied color to her face with a brush. Finally, they nodded their approval and held up a jewel-encrusted mirror for Mara to see the results of their handiwork.

She gasped.

Her skin glowed, and her lips blazed with the same shade of red as the rubies at her throat. Her blue eyes matched the sapphires threaded through her elaborate updo. The red undertones in her hair seemed richer in the chamber's light.

She swallowed hard. Was this who she was? Was this who Adrian wished her to be? She looked like an untouchable movie star or real-life princess, not a kindergarten teacher from Michigan who usually had paste on her blouse.

The women waited anxiously for her reaction. Mara forced herself to smile and nod at them. Giggling, they left, almost running into the woman entering the chamber. She wore a purple gown, and her hair, swept into a simple but elegant chignon, was the same sandy blonde as Adrian's. Her face was unlined, except for dimples in her cheeks when she smiled. Green eyes, like Adrian's, sparkled as she took Mara's hand and gently squeezed it. "I'm Nitia. Adrian's mother, my sister. Adrian's father, like you, lived on land."

"Where?" Mara asked. But when Nitia looked puzzled, Mara rephrased, calling upon her kindergarten teacher's skills. "From where? What place did he live? What city?"

Nitia smiled with understanding. "Tahiti."

"Adrian didn't tell me," Mara said.

Nitia's smile faded. "Adrian very sad. His mother and father perish. Torpedo."

Mara tried to stop the tears spilling down her cheeks, not wanting to spoil the ladies' handiwork.

Nitia wiped the moisture away with a swatch of soft linen. "I see you love Adrian," she said.

Mara nodded. "But why does he want me here?" she asked. "I'm ordinary. And I'm afraid of the water." At Nitia's confused look, Mara tried again. "Adrian chose me, why? Why not lady with sea form?"

Nitia's giggle was lilting and musical, causing Mara to join in. "Adrian, your..." She used the same musical language Adrian had. "It is scribed in hall of records. You and Adrian, twin flames." She lowered her voice then. "Almost time. Watch Lorion. He wants Adrian to rule with another, not his twin flame." She stroked Mara's cheek. "But Adrian stubborn like mother and brave like father."

"Brave?" Mara asked.

Nitia stood up, and Mara followed. "Adrian's father leave to warn of torpedoes. Sister show him the way. I watch over Adrian."

"How do you know they perished?" Mara asked.

Nitia reached her hand toward the array of crystal on the table. "Crystals, we see and hear words on land."

"How? Show me," Mara said.

Nitia lifted a crystal in the shape of a wand and pressed it gently above the bridge of Mara's nose. Images and words played through her mind like a movie, although the sound wasn't quite with the pictures. It was Gary and Jana, and they were in Mara's apartment in Michigan.

"It's from the school district," Jana said. "It looks important. Should we open it?"

Gary frowned. "Her cell phone just goes to voice mail."

"It's thin," Jana said. "It would be a thicker envelope if it was her contract, wouldn't it?"

Mara sighed. No tenure. She was disappointed but not surprised.

Nitia placed the crystal back with a small smile. "It is time."

Chapter 5

In the great hall, Adrian waited for Mara to appear. Lorion, Adrian's Aunt Nitia, and the others, would witness the affirmation of their third joining. Then Lorion, the acting regent and chosen leader of the elders, would say the ancient words so he and Mara could rule the Crystal City after they returned from their journey back to land. Only then would Adrian take the mantle of leadership.

The chamber opened and she appeared—beautiful, although she shook with nerves. Adrian fought his urge to run to her side and reassure her. It was written that she must come to him and stay with him of her own volition.

She clutched a single cana lily, the same shade of red as her delectable lips. Her beautiful blue eyes, the color of the sea on a cloudless day, darted nervously over all the room.

Adrian watched her hesitant steps. *Look at me*, he entreated silently.

She lifted her head and met his gaze, her steps faltering.

Come to me, he urged.

She stood frozen. His heart thundered in his chest. He was asking too much of her. Her life would be so different from everything she had known. She would essentially be dead to her loved ones. From under the waves in the Crystal City she would only be able to communicate telepathically with humans bearing enlightened minds. While she could continue to walk on land, she wouldn't age as humans did. Something which would raise fear and suspicion among the humans and put those who dwelled in the Crystal City and other places beneath the riptides at great risk. And, as his parents' deaths proved, the journey through the waves to land held peril and death.

He knew she felt great anguish at her separation from her mother. How could he ask this of her? He'd rushed her into the sea. Although she seemed delighted with her sea form, the thought of her taking food the humans called lunch, with that scribe who put his hands on her, had addled Adrian's brain and caused him to react rashly.

He swallowed hard. He had promised to take her back. If they joined now, and she didn't return under the sea with him, he would forfeit his right to rule. Still, he would marry no other. Mara was his. Yet if he forced her to stand beside him in the Crystal City as his wife and lady, when she yearned for her loved ones and her life above the riptides, her essence would shrivel. He couldn't bear that. Nor could he bear not binding her to him irrevocably, while he had the chance.

Mara, my heart, he called her name silently, the melody echoing with his conflicted heart.

ՀԶՀԶ

Mara smiled and walked across the great hall to where he stood. Words in Adrian's language began to fill the air and sounded similar to those spoken in the ceremony she'd dreamed.

Was any of this real?

The man Nitia called Lorion glared at Adrian for a quick moment. When Lorion caught her watching, he eased his features into a haughty expression.

Adrian took her free hand and kept firm hold while a woman with flowing white hair, smooth face, and clear sharp hazel eyes read from a scroll. Mara noted her feet were wide and weblike. Mara's stomach rumbled and embarrassment flared. Everyone near would have heard her. What did they eat here?

She hadn't seen or smelled food since she'd arrived. She'd been a meat and potatoes girl, and never eaten a lot of seafood. The thought had her suppressing an inappropriate giggle.

Adrian squeezed her hand, his beautiful eyes full of concern. The woman stopped speaking and set the scroll down. Adrian stared into Mara's eyes, smiled, and said, "Forever, it is done."

All her earlier anxiety disappeared as he watched her expectantly. His stare penetrated into her soul. How could he love an ordinary woman, afraid of the water?

Adrian smiled and shook his head, ever so slightly. He saw her more clearly than anyone, she knew. He saw who she was and he loved her anyway. The surety of it sank deep into her bones, although he'd never said the words in English.

Her world shifted in that instant. She loved him. She belonged to him, with him, wherever that was. The words came from her lips, the truest she'd ever spoken. "Forever, darling."

Adrian's eyes blazed with joy. "It is done."

He pulled her into his arms and fused his lips to hers for a too-brief kiss then took hold of her and left the great hall. Her feet barely found purchase on the smooth marble floors, as they dashed to a private chamber where a sumptuous banquet awaited.

Shellfish, grapes, and crisp juicy slices of what looked like fruit- and vegetable-type bites she'd never seen before filled a low glass-like table. Her eyes widened.

"Mara?" Adrian looked panicked and pointed at the shellfish. "You are ill from that food?"

"No," she said. "I'm not allergic."

Relief wiped the panic from his face, and he gathered her into his arms until her cheek nestled against his broad shoulder. He released her when her stomach rumbled.

"So much food," she pointed to the feast. "Just for us?"

His lips quirked into a quick smile. He settled her on cushions on a large circular mattress so she was sitting up, then he turned to where the food lay. He returned with a flat piece of what resembled petrified driftwood, polished smooth and piled high with food. He sat close, their legs brushing, and set the plate beside them.

Would they eat from the same plate? Did they use utensils? Would he use his fingers? She was hungry for food, knowledge, and him—and not necessarily in that order. But a girl had to eat. Before she could ask, he deftly lifted a piece of shrimp to her lips with marble chopsticks before he took some for himself.

Chewing, she considered the taste. She'd had raw sushi before but this seemed cooked. "How do you make food here?"

He fed her a crunchy vegetable before he answered. "Crystal City…" He paused, obviously searching for the words. "…has knowledge of all technology of humans, and what you do not know yet." He fed her a bite of oyster in a tangy sauce then took one for himself.

"So you are saying you are more advanced here?" she asked.

He nodded.

"What about disease?" Her eyes grew wide in panic. "What if I brought human disease to you?" Her breath felt strangled in her chest. "A disease you have no resistance to?" She felt ill. Scrambling away from him, she began to pace around the chamber. Her father and brother were physicians, so she should know better. She bit her lip hard. How could she have been so thoughtless? Her rash actions could wipe out the Crystal City and kill Adrian.

He was at her side and took hold of her shoulders.

She shook him off and stepped back to face him. Tears streamed down her cheeks. "Don't touch me, Adrian."

His eyes changed to a stormy gray she'd never seen before.

"I could make you ill, sick with human disease, if I haven't already," she sobbed.

"Mara." His voice held the bite of command, but he made no move to touch her.

She balled her hands into fists, feeling her fingernails pierce her palms, causing blood to seep.

"Not happen, ever," he said. "We are with humans before." Her sobs subsided, and he took a step closer. "My father human."

She'd forgotten that. Hope bloomed in her heart.

"Your disease not hurt us and, I—" He stopped as if considering his words. "We not hurt Mara."

He took her hands, wiping a gentle finger over the smears of blood on her palms. He drew her toward a table of crystals and moved one. The two ladies who'd arranged her hair re-appeared. Adrian said something in their language, and Mara only recognized the words for "disease" and "afraid."

The two ladies left the chamber, only to return and rubbed balm into Mara's palms while Adrian held her. The ladies murmured musical chants, stroked her cheeks, and wiped away her tears. They gave her sweet smiles and then left.

Mara looked at her palms. No trace of her scratches remained.

"I'm sorry, darling." She watched his eyes blaze at her endearment. "There's so much I don't understand."

Relief mixed with humor, adding a teasing glint to his eyes. "I teach you, darling."

Chapter 6

Mara caressed Adrian's handsome face, as he pressed a kiss to her palm, Shivers flowed over her arms. "And you teach me."

He smiled.

Her heart raced. Would he always affect her like this?

He drew her to the cushions, sat, and tugged her down until her back was against his chest. Then he lifted a quartz crystal to her forehead.

Once again the sound was out of sync with the images, like a dubbed movie. She giggled. His body relaxed and she melted into him. As the scenes played in her mind, she realized it was translated into English from Adrian's language, much like a film you would show to schoolchildren about life in another country. This time the country was the Crystal City.

As she shut her eyes to process the images, he fed her bits of food. She sucked his fingers after one succulent morsel of lobster and heard his sharp intake of breath. He hardened against her. The images continued, showing children in a classroom learning the geography of the bottom of the sea and how human pollution was altering that environment.

Depressed, she sighed. "We're ruining everything."

His mouth was close to her ear. "No, darling."

Could he see and hear the same images? Or was it, as she wondered before, that he could read her thoughts?

"Only if you wish it," he said, feeding her a slice of sweet, juicy fruit, perhaps citrus?

Holy hell. Could everyone read everyone else's thoughts here? Did they all know everything she was thinking?

She licked his fingers clean, taking exquisite time and care to complete the task. He growled and untied her sash, then his own, before tossing them both aside. When he unfastened something, her gown slipped off her shoulders. He took the crystal away from her forehead and pressed his lips to her neck. She sighed. His hands moved to cup her breasts and she arched her spine toward him to give him access.

"Mara," he whispered.

"Please, Adrian," she moaned. Was that her voice?

He chuckled. Within seconds, she was naked beneath him. He teased her nipples into hard, needy nubs before his hand strayed lower.

She opened her legs to him. "Adrian, please," she begged. Who was she?

His eyes blazed into hers as his fingers touched her feminine core. "Mine," he growled.

"Yours," she said. "Forever, it is done." Unbidden, the words sprang from her lips.

She wrapped her fingers around his hard shaft. He groaned.

"My darling," she whispered when he seemed hesitant to enter her. She tried to search his hazy thoughts. Hadn't he said something about getting her pregnant? That it wasn't possible on land, only here?

"Oh," she said.

Using all her strength, she rolled him underneath her body and kissed his neck, working her way down to his erection. She took him in her mouth, unsure how this went. She'd never done this, but she had a general idea of how it was done from snippets her friends had shared.

He groaned and held her head gently, so she guessed she was on the right path. She took him into her mouth, scraping him lightly with her teeth and eliciting a moan. Sucking him hard, she felt pressure building in his balls as she palmed them gently.

"Mara," his voice held a warning.

Ignoring it, she took him full into her mouth and breathed deep to suppress her gag reflex as he surged into her. She swallowed hard. He lifted her and stared at her in wonder. He kissed her then, his tongue delving deep. She shuddered. He broke off the kiss and caressed her cheek.

"Mara, mine, you surprise me." Desire lit his eyes. He tumbled her over and spread her legs wide. His tongue stroked deep within her folds, tasting her while his thumb teased her, bringing her close to her release. Only then did he move his fingers inside to her sweet spot.

"Adrian," she begged him.

He chuckled as she thrashed on the cushions. His fingers found her sensitive nub again. "What is it, darling?"

She whimpered. He used his mouth and she exploded, screaming as waves of pleasure crashed through her like the riptide. Her scant experience—one guy in college—had been nothing close to this.

He held her in his arms. Her head rested on his chest and she fell asleep to the sound of his heartbeat.

❦

Adrian positioned the crystals so they would not be disturbed. Mara stirred softly against him and he stilled, not wishing to disturb her. He wanted nothing more than to bury himself inside her. The final part of their joining would be here, home in Crystal City, when she accepted the possibility of children.

His kind joined forever. He had waited for ages to claim her. She had remembered he could only make her pregnant here, but she obviously wasn't ready. How long would it take? He had to learn her language better.

Her hair had come loose from the style she'd worn for the ceremony. He worked the strands free with his fingers and she sighed. He made note to remember that she liked that.

He felt her come awake as he combed his fingers through her hair. She looked up at him and smiled. He forced himself to breathe. Did she know how beautiful she was? Or how her eyes sparkled blue like the seas under a cloudless sky? He grew hard and moved away from her. There was no protection he could use here to prevent a baby if she didn't wish it. He stifled a groan and slipped his loincloth over his protesting erection.

"Adrian?"

He turned toward her. The ruby necklace nestled between her perfect breasts. He longed to suck on her nipples until she screamed his name again. He tore his eyes away to look at her face, set with lines of determination. "Yes, darling?"

She smiled at that and he twitched beneath his loincloth. She would be his undoing. "I want to learn your language," she said.

He took her hand, helped her out of bed, and dressed her in the robe she'd worn for the ceremony. "Easier for me to learn more English words." He moved the quartz crystals to summon food. They had not eaten much last night.

"How many languages do you know?" she asked.

He paused. "*Seis*, six." He kissed the tip of her nose. "Some of them no longer spoken."

"Oh," she said. "You know Spanish?"

"Not as much as I want," he said.

"I took two years in high school and three semesters in college." She lifted her chin and turned to face him. "I want to learn your language, Adrian, I mean it."

He smiled into her eyes. "You will, *querida*, I promise."

She rushed into his arms. Did she know how she tempted him? He was helpless to resist her. He kissed her, and she darted her tongue into his mouth as she rubbed against his erection.

He moved his mouth to the shell of her ear. "Mara." His voice held a question.

She pressed against him. "Please, Adrian."

He took her face in his hands. "You know what you ask?" He ground his mouth onto hers for a brief, punishing kiss. When he lifted his head, her lips were swollen. He sucked hard on her breasts, knowing it would leave a mark. "My baby inside you?'

"Yes," she nodded. "I love you. *Te amo.*"

He moved them to the cushions and knocked over the crystal to seal the chamber from any intrusions.

Love, she said she loved him. That word didn't begin to describe his feelings for her. He ripped off her gown and kissed her everywhere, lapsing into his native tongue. She'd released his erection from his loincloth when the wailing chants began. He stilled.

Beneath him, she tensed. "What's wrong?" she whispered.

He sat up, dragging her with him. He kissed her forehead and took a deep breath. "Something bad."

Her face paled.

Chapter 7

Adrian donned his white robe then slipped Mara's over her head. He made quick work of tying the gold sashes around their waists. Holding her close, his expression grim, he led her into a cavern-like space she hadn't seen before. People in various colored robes filled the cavernous space. Formations of minerals hung from the high ceiling.

The High Council gathered on a raised area. The crowd parted, allowing Adrian and Mara through. They climbed granite steps until they faced the waiting Council.

Lorion bristled at Adrian's presence and aimed a

hate-filled glare at Mara. She shivered and Adrian drew her closer.

He snapped out something in his language.

Lorion answered, Adrian stiffened, tucking her even closer to him, as if worried she'd be snatched away. Nitia came to their side.

"Quake on the sea floor," she said. "Make wave. Hit land."

Why did Lorion look at her with such hatred as if it was her fault? Mara drew on Adrian's strength and Nitia's loving, calm composure. She listened carefully to the ensuing argument between Adrian and Lorion. From what she could gather, anyone who could be spared from Crystal City and the other cities under the riptides were needed to assess and stem any damage to the aquatic systems and reefs.

Nitia placed her soft hand to Mara's cheek. "You stay with Nitia, wait for Adrian?"

Mara stole a look at Lorion. He was watching their exchange. She shuddered and turned her back to him.

"I take you back," Adrian said. His smile was sad. "To land, then bring you back with me to Crystal City, if you wish it."

"Could I stay with you and help?" Even as she asked, she knew she would be more of a hindrance, rather than a help. Nitia's hand stroked her shoulders that had turned stiff with nerves.

"Darling." Adrian gathered her into his arms, then

drew back to caress her cheek. "Mine," he said, staring into her eyes.

"Yours." Mara gave him a smile. His grim mood needed a lift.

"We go," he said.

Mara hugged Nitia. "Thank you for welcoming me with such kindness."

Nitia looked puzzled. Adrian translated until Nitia smiled and pointed to her heart.

"She says *por nada*, you're welcome." He nuzzled her ear then brought her to a chamber where steps led down to seawater. Stripping them both of their robes, he then sat on the steps with his legs submerged. His sea form took shape.

"Come, Mara."

She sat on the steps and dangled her legs in the seawater. Nothing happened.

"Adrian?" Disappointed, she looked at him. Humor lit his eyes and she sighed with relief. After the news of the quake, she worried he would lose that joy she loved so much.

"Only if I wish, Mara." He kissed her hard. She opened her mouth, greedy for his taste. He lifted his lips. "Until we join here, only when I wish it."

"Control freak." She felt the tingling start in her feet then move up. In brilliant hues of blues and orange, her tail came first. She squealed in joy, feeling complete.

His hands went to the ruby necklace.

"Should I take it off?" she said.

He looked alarmed. "No." He touched the stones glittering in the valley of her breasts. "You wear it always."

"Okay," she said.

He kissed her again and pulled her under. Once under the waves, he swam powerfully, confident in their course and sustaining her oxygen supply. Without him, she wouldn't survive. She came up for air, suddenly afraid. What if something happened to him on the long swim back? Would she want to live without him? No. Her heart wrenched at the thought of a world without him.

Adrian surfaced next to her, staying close. "It is the same for me." His gaze was intense. "And I keep you safe."

"How?" she asked.

He smiled. "We are joined, mostly."

She knew they had to leave, but she had a couple of more questions. "When we join here, will I take sea form when I wish? Will I know what you are thinking?"

"You know now," he answered.

She put her hands on his shoulders. Waves of feeling enveloped her. She could feel his love and longing for her, like nothing she'd ever known. There was pride woven within, pride that she was his. She didn't bristle at his possessiveness, instead reveled in it, because he belonged to her, too.

"When we return, we rule Crystal City."

How could she rule with him? "Adrian, I don't know how."

He silenced her with another deep kiss. She sighed into his mouth, loving the way he tasted.

cↄeↄ

Adrian kept her close as he took her back to the island the humans called Hawaii. He stopped more often than needed, taking time to kiss her and ensure she had breath under the waves. It didn't help that he couldn't get enough of her.

Would he ever? Even after she learned to breathe under the waves in her sea form, he would always stop to kiss her. She couldn't see underwater yet, but in time her beautiful blue eyes would adapt. He couldn't wait to share his favorite coral reefs and sacred seas, where dolphins and whales gave birth, with her.

Would she always delight him so much? Did she know this had been her destiny? How would she handle parting from her human loved ones? Did she know how much she was already loved in the Crystal City? Even the old windbag Lorion seemed to grudgingly accept her. Remembering how Lorion looked at her sent a vague uneasiness prickling through him.

Adrian stopped to kiss her again, uncaring that he was prolonging this journey while his duties waited. He had waited so long for her. She came to him so sweetly and trusting each time. How could he leave her? The closer they drew to the island, the stronger his panic grew. He could lose her. He cursed his duties, but he could never forsake them.

He seized her waist in a vice-like grip as he propelled them through the last riptide. Finally, he let her go to swim on her own. She shook her tail at him, and he caught her close for another kiss.

∽∾∽

Mara loved him. She'd loved him in her dreams, before he came to claim her. Adrian let go of her, and she realized her tail was gone. They were near the beach in Kauai where they first met. He used his strong arms to pull himself through the shallows and up onto the sand.

It was dark. The sun just slipping over the horizon. She sat next to him in the wet sand until Adrian changed from his sea form. Naked, they ran laughing to her timeshare. How could she let him leave her? She wanted him with every cell in her body.

"Darling?"

He smiled at her endearment.

"Can we come back on land, after I join with you in Crystal City?"

Feeling shy, she lowered her gaze and saw proof that he wanted her.

He moved her wet hair aside and nuzzled her neck until she melted against him. "Yes, at times."

His palm cradled her cheek. She kissed it, desperate for his taste. He thickened against her and she groaned, grinding against him, mindless with need.

He was breathing hard. "You will not age as others on land." He lifted her and she wrapped her legs around his waist. "You will look the same as others on land age."

Distantly she processed what he was telling her. Gary and Jana would notice. And that would put Adrian and the others like him in danger. She kissed him, as he thrust inside her.

She tore her mouth away from. She had to know. "Will it always be like this for us? "

His lips twitched into a quick smile. "No."

She gasped.

"Is better under the waves." He plunged into her hard and fast without the restraint he'd shown before, hitting a spot inside her she never knew existed. She came fast, screaming his name, just before he emptied himself inside her. Her tears fell and he kissed them away, murmuring her name.

How could that be better in Crystal City?

"It will," he said. Sadness clouded his eyes.

She blinked hard to stop her tears, and tried to twist her face into a smile. "You have to go."

He kissed her tenderly then eased away from her.

"Let me find you something to wear to the beach."

She stifled a hiccup, trying to hold back her sobs, and turned on the TV. She turned away and found a pair of gray stretch shorts in her bedroom.

He pulled them on. Dressed, he took her in his arms and tucked her head under his chin. His heartbeat thundered, while hers felt like it was breaking. He dragged them toward the door then stopped.

"I'm coming with you to the beach." She searched for something to cover her nakedness.

He shook his head and took hold of the ruby necklace. "No, darling." His hands cupped her breasts then strayed lower. She melted into his touch.

"…breaking news! A tidal wave, possibly of tsunami proportions, has been detected in the South Pacific and could possibly strike the coast of New Zealand…" The TV announcer's words ripped them apart.

He grabbed hold of her necklace, his face grim. "Mine, Mara." His gaze was fierce as it raked over her.

She swallowed hard and nodded. "Yes, darling. Yours, only yours."

He seemed to relax a bit.

"How long will it take?" she asked.

"I take you back as soon as I can. Has to be before next big moon."

"Why?"

He didn't answer her.

"Will you come to me when I sleep?" She dropped her gaze, ashamed she sounded so weak and needy.

He put his hand under her chin and forced her to look into his eyes. "No."

Tears streamed down her cheeks. She wiped them away. Wanting him to remember her smiling, not weeping, she took long, deep breaths.

"I come for you here."

He ground his mouth down on hers and she felt him harden. She slipped her hand under his shorts and caressed him. He sighed and shut his eyes. He opened them, and mischief lit them, making them nearly gold. "Is good my sea form will hide how you make me hard."

He turned and left. She gave into the sobs until she fell into a fitful sleep.

Chapter 8

It was daytime when Mara opened her eyes, alone in the tiny timeshare. Was it days or hours ago, when she'd been deliriously happy? Or had she just been delirious? What day was it? How much time had passed? The TV droned away, but there was nothing about a tsunami or tidal wave on any channel.

Had it all been a dream? Was Adrian real? Was she delusional? If she was, she had no business teaching children. Maybe her cranky principal was right not to offer tenure. She lifted her hair off her neck. Her skin was sticky with sweat and salt water, and something lay at the base of her throat.

Rushing to the mirror, she studied the gleaming red stones. Adrian's words to wear it always, echoed in her head. She held it tightly and spun in giddy circles in front of the TV.

He was real. He was gone.

She stopped, feeling nauseous, and sank to the cushions on the couch, realizing she wasn't wearing a stitch of clothing. Her cell phone was on the coffee table. She picked it up to figure out what day it was. Holy cow. Three days had passed.

The phone had ten messages, eight from Gary and two from Mike. Listening to the messages, she winced. In the first message, Mike was ticked off, only to become worried in the later one. She texted *Soooo sorry. My bad. I'm okay. Don't blame u for being pissed.*

A minute after she hit send, the phone rang. It was Mike.

"I'm not pissed. But you can make it up to me if you meet me for lunch."

Her stomach rumbled. She was starving. "Sure," she said.

He gave her the name of the place, Zeke's, and directions.

She dialed Gary's cell phone next. He was with their mother and beyond angry at Mara.

"Let me talk to mom," Mara said. "I'll explain later."

"Here, Mom, it's Mara," Gary said.

"Who is Mara?" her mother asked, her voice as sweet as ever.

"Hi, Mom." Mara fought back tears and tried to keep her voice cheerful. "I'm in Hawaii, remember?"

"What's Hawaii?"

"The tropical island. I'm here for my vacation, because school's out," Mara patiently explained.

"School?"

Mara wiped tears from her cheeks and decided to change the topic. "What did you eat today?"

Her mother recited everything she ate and said it was raining outside.

"I love you, Mom," Mara said.

Gary took back the phone. "Call me later. I'm late for my shift. Be safe, bug."

Mara hit end and smiled at Gary's nickname, given because she was major pest when they were kids, always following him around whenever he'd let her. If she joined with Adrian in Crystal City, would she ever see Gary again? Would she be able to be auntie to the kids he and Jana wanted so desperately?

Yes, they would.

They would find a way.

Glancing at herself in her mirror, she winced at her puffy, red eyes. Guess she would be keeping her sunglasses on during her lunch with Mike. Surely the place had outside seating. She grabbed her sunglasses and stemmed her tears with firm resolve.

☙❧☙

Adrian swam toward the reef Lorion had assigned him, barely noticing the caves and shipwrecks he longed to show Mara. He hadn't thought the reef he'd been assigned to bore checking. It was so far away from the place the humans named New Zealand. The quake hadn't been as strong as feared. Unlike the previous wall of waves that struck land in years past, there was nothing to be seen or felt in these depths. This was a likely a fool's errand, but it wouldn't do to disobey the last order the old windbag would give him.

He missed Mara with every cell of his being.

Damn his duty. This time with Mara was what the humans called a honeymoon. Did she miss him as much as he missed her? He hadn't had time to explain that she was somewhat altered after he allowed her to take sea form. A necessary change that allowed him to know her thoughts if she were near him, critical for communicating when they were in the depths. But it meant he couldn't come to her when she slept, nor would he be able to read her thoughts when she was on land and he was in the sea.

He only had seven land days, while the moon shone whole, to get back to her. After that the riptides would be too strong to breach with Mara in tow. It was also when the governance of Crystal City would pass to him, per the treaty, so long as his he and his life-mate were fully joined.

What was worrisome was they hadn't gotten that far. The treaty with the other cities beneath the riptides stipulated that the regent, which was now Lorion, would maintain his duties or appoint someone else to do so, if Adrian failed to appear.

It was no secret the old windbag wanted his weak-willed son Romian to govern. Romian would be his father's puppet and join with a mate from beneath the riptides. Lorion had pressured Adrian to seek his mate from one of the cities in the alliance.

Yet, once Nitia had taken Adrian into the Hall of Records, he looked into the crystals and saw the one destined to be his, Mara.

Nitia called him determined, much like his parents. They had dared to challenge the existing Crystal City law forbidding the joining with humans. In fact, his parents amended the law with the caveat that humans must choose to join their beings with those who took sea form of their own free will.

A ruler on his homeland above the waves, Adrian's father had joined with his mother to live in the sea, with no promise he would have a voice in any of the politics governing Crystal City.

Adrian's mother had held the position of governor, leaving Adrian's father as her beloved, trusted advisor.

Nitia had shared with Adrian that, although his father loved his mother beyond reason, his duty to the humans compelled him to swim through dangerous waters to his homeland and warn them of the impending war he discovered written in the Hall of Records.

His father set out alone through the depths to bring the message to his people. His mother, sick with concern for her beloved's safety, tore herself away from the son they loved so much to find her mate as he swam beneath the riptides. She wanted to ensure his safety on such a futile mission. His parents' warning had saved the lives of many humans, but they had perished in the crossfire of a torpedo attack.

If placed in his father's position, would he be strong enough to leave everything he knew to be with the one he loved? He'd be stranded on land, as ignorant of humans' ways as his father had been of life in Crystal City.

No. His sea form required the vibration of pure water beneath the waves. While he could survive above the waves for half a moon's waxing, he would always have to leave her. Being parted from her now made him almost ill.

He approached the reef he'd been assigned to assess. The damage was worse than feared. The volcano on the sea floor, which had triggered the mountain of water, had disrupted the ecosystem sustaining the reef.

Centering his life force, he transmitted the message through the depths to sea forms inhabiting the underwater cities. He couldn't handle this alone. Unfortunately, since he had discovered this, it was his responsibility to stay until work to restore the area to minimal order was done.

Dread filled him. Such an undertaking would put him perilously close to the fat moon.

❧❧

Mara ordered the coconut shrimp and pulled out her cell phone while Mike answered an urgent text message from the copy desk at his newspaper.

"Sorry, I thought I was through edits," he muttered, not taking his attention away from his phone.

She smiled and continued to search "next full moon in July" on the restaurant's Internet connection on her cell phone. She assumed that's what Adrian meant by fat moon. She loved his odd turn of phrases. She would have to learn the language spoken in the Crystal City. Would they think she was as inept as her principal did? What would she do there? Adrian couldn't fill every minute of her time, as delicious as that would be.

"Holy hell," Mike said. "Excuse me. I have to talk my nervous editor."

He headed toward the parking lot and away from the bustle of the crowded restaurant. It was loud, even where they sat outside. She looked toward the fully stocked bar, jammed with people, and the carved, wooden mermaid hanging alongside a fisherman's net.

She glanced down at her phone and slipped her sunglasses off to see the screen on her cell phone better. One week—the moon waxed full in one week. Adrian said they had to be back in Crystal City by then, but he hadn't said why.

Panic surged through her. How could she wrap up her life in a week? Adrian said they could come back, but it would raise suspicions. Mainly because she wouldn't age as others on land. Besides, his parents had died on such a trip, which didn't bode well for the two of them. She signaled the waitress. Ordering a concoction of rum and pineapple juice, she asked for it extra strong.

Mike sat back down. "Sorry." His eyebrows shot up in concern. "You've been crying."

Crap. She slipped her sunglasses back on, but he moved to take her hand. She snatched it away, and put it in her lap.

He frowned. "What's wrong Mara?"

Her drink arrived and she took a gulp. The smell made her queasy, so she set it down and pushed it toward him.

Mike put his straw into her glass. "Don't mind if I do," he said, tasting it. "One of Zeke's deadly doubles." He watched her steadily, ignoring his cell phone which kept pinging with email messages.

"I met someone." She looked around the room to avoid Mike's scrutiny, her gaze landing once again on the wooden mermaid. Perfect. She grimaced.

"Here?" he asked. "You met someone since you got here?"

She nodded, fighting down waves of nausea.

"Holy hell." He took a long sip of her drink.

"Don't you have to go back to work?" she said.

He said a rude word. "Take those glasses off so I can see your face, please."

She raised a shaky hand and removed her sunglasses.

"You look beautiful, by the way, aside from the puffy, swollen eyes. That necklace suits you." He took a long drink of his ice water. "Who is he?"

Her hand went to her throat. "Adrian, his name is Adrian."

"Adrian what?"

Crap. This was a bad idea. Mike would know everyone on this island.

"He's not from here."

"Mara, what is the man's last name?"

She leaned in to take a sip of the pineapple concoction, and fought back the bile that rose in her throat.

He frowned at her silence. "So, what you're saying, is you don't know the guy's last name."

"I don't know your last name." She fought to keep her voice calm. "And you don't know mine, either."

"Jeffries, Mike Jeffries."

"Mine's Cunningham," she said.

"Where is he from?"

Thankfully their food came and she ignored his question, tucking into her coconut shrimp until it was gone. It seemed to recharge her. She'd never been that wild about shellfish before. But she was still hungry.

The waitress came back with a look of kind concern. "You need anything else, honey?"

"Another order, please?" she asked in a small voice.

"He didn't feed you, either," Mike grumbled.

Remembering Adrian holding her between his legs and feeding her morsels of food with his fingers set off a different kind of hunger. She hadn't been hungry for food then, only him.

Her face grew hot, probably coloring as crimson as the rubies.

Mike said another rude word.

She shifted uncomfortably in her chair, and then looked him squarely in the eye, sick of his pissy attitude. "You're a great guy, Mike. I can't believe you're not seeing someone."

He rolled his eyes.

"But what I need right now is a friend. I'm here short-term anyway." When, not if, Adrian came for her, she'd be gone. "Tell me about the mermaid."

Mike looked startled. "What?"

She pointed to the wooden beauty hanging above the bar.

He looked vaguely uncomfortable. "A legend in the islands, first recorded in English when Europeans sailed from Tahiti to Hawaii." He pronounced Hawaii with a V.

Her second order arrived, and the waitress beamed at her. "Zeke said it's on the house since you have the good taste to appreciate his signature dish."

"Thanks." Mara scanned the crowded restaurant for Zeke.

"By the bar," Mike said. "The guy with the beard."

Zeke's long gray hair was tied back in a ponytail. He wore a long beard and black Harley shirt. He lifted a glass to acknowledge her then turned to speak with someone.

"What's the legend?" Mara tucked into her shrimp.

"More often female, usually depicted like her." Mike pointed to the carving.

Mara studied it closer. The expression on the mermaid's face conveyed she was unbothered by her bare breasts. A thick, chunky necklace rendered in excellent detail in the wood, was a similar to the rubies Mara wore around her neck. She finished the last bite of shrimp and swallowed hard. She longed so fiercely for her sea form, remembering her glorious tail, alive in hues of blues and oranges.

The rain that soaked the isles every day started. Mara inhaled the smell of the pure water and calmed. A curious tingling started in her feet. A rivulet of water from the downpour soaked her bare toes. She nearly squealed in joy, but carefully lifted her feet from the tiny puddle.

"We should be dry here." Mike stared wistfully at the mermaid over the bar. "You know, your name means truth in Japanese, and water in the romance languages. How did a kid from the Midwest wind up with a name like that?"

She laughed. "I'm from Michigan, Mike. Have you heard of the Great Lakes? We grew up surrounded by water. My dad was good at languages. He used his GI Bill to help with med school. He was stationed all over."

Mike grinned. "I've only been to California on the mainland. Who's we?"

She stared at him in confusion.

"You said we grew up."

"Gary, my older brother, I pestered the hell out of him growing up. He's a doc like Dad." Tears welled. She would likely never see her brother or sweet, kind Jana again. Or her mother. Her mother had been her father's whole world, which could explain why her sweet mother's mind had collapsed so quickly without him.

Mara was doing the same thing. Adrian was her whole world. She would be lost in Crystal City.

No, she decided, she would find a way to be useful. Adrian's father had found a way, so would she. But what if she lost him, as her mother had lost her own husband? What would become of her beneath the rip tides?

"Dessert?" asked the waitress.

Mara longed to sink her teeth into more shrimp, but smiled and said no.

Mike stared at the mermaid over the bar, frowning.

"Mike?" Mara prompted.

"Oh." He shook his head. "No thanks."

She and Mike planned to meet for dinner the next day, and he would text with directions. She would go, if she was still here. They said their goodbyes.

She sat in her car, calculated the time difference back in Michigan, and dialed her mother's number. She took a big gulp of water from the bottle she'd brought with her as the call went through. Her throat felt scratchy and sore from all her weeping. She choked back more tears when she heard her mother's sweet, tentative, hello. "It's Mara, Mom."

"How's my baby?"

Mara's hope soared. Was her mother lucid?

"Gary said you're on vacation. I'm so glad. You work so hard."

Mara forced her words past the lump in her throat. How could she not be there to see the recognition on her mother's face? Tears coursed down her cheeks. "It's beautiful here. You would love the flowers and the ocean, Mom."

"I saw you in the Crystal place, dear."

Mara gasped.

"You looked so beautiful. Your father would be so proud. And your husband, he adores you."

Mara's chest felt tight. She forced herself to breathe in and out like she and her friend, Kristen, had learned in yoga class.

"You must be with him, baby," her mother said. "It's your destiny."

"Mom?" Mara heard Gary's voice. Had he heard what her mother said? "Can I talk to Mara for a minute?"

Crap.

"Hey Mar."

"Hey Gar." She sobbed at their use of their rhyming nicknames.

"Take it easy, bug. We were having a great day until now."

She took huge gulps of air and tried to stay calm. They set up a time to Skype, then Gary handed the phone over to their mother.

"I love you, Mom, so much," Mara said.

"Love you, too," her mother said.

Chapter 9

Mara drove to the spot where she'd first met Mike and seen Adrian. She took the long walk down to the beach. It was almost deserted. A posted sign read *Dangerous Undertow*.

She stepped toward the sea, sat down on the slightly wet sand, and stuck her feet in the ocean, waiting. The Pacific churned. Her feet tingled in the salt water and she squealed, but the surf drowned her voice out.

Her tail, resplendent in the orange and blue hues she adored, fluttered to life. She sighed.

"Adrian?" she called toward the waves.

A head popped up out of the water. Her heart raced.

"Adrian?" she called again and tried to see the swimmer's features.

Her hope plummeted as the swimmer emerged from the sea on the crest of a large wave. A flash of bare breasts confirmed it wasn't Adrian.

Mara kept her tail submerged, her panic noticeably absent. Instead, a peaceful calm settled in every cell of her being. Her tail was temporary, and her land feet would come back when she was dry. An odd sadness that she wasn't wholly Adrian's to command with regard to her sea form seeped through her. But she loved her tail and fluttered it in the water.

Absently, she wondered what would happen when she bathed or showered.

The beach was empty as the nude swimmer came closer to shore. Enough so Mara could see her necklace, similar in style to Mara's, but set with dark green stones. The redhead swam in the shallows and smiled with joy when she saw Mara's tail. She hoisted herself on the beach with well-toned arms. Her tail was glittering in hues of red and green. She settled next to Mara in the sand and tugged at the black T-shirt Mara wore, giggling, unconcerned about her own bare breasts. She fingered Mara's necklace and raised her eyebrows in question.

"You human?"

Mara nodded. "Yes."

"I'm Cerissa."

"I'm Mara."

Cerissa's eyes widened. "Adrian's Mara, from Crystal City?"

Mara squared her shoulders. "Yes." She looked around, checking that they were still alone. She touched Cerissa's arm and tried to speak over the knot in her throat. "Adrian is safe?"

"It is not known." Cerissa chose her next words with great care. "You love him?"

Tears welled up in Mara's eyes. All she could manage was a nod.

"Then why you eat with Mike?"

"You know Mike?" Mara couldn't believe it.

Cerissa nodded.

"We're just friends. We ate shrimp." Mara pulled her tail out of the water and felt the tingling that signaled the return of her feet. "Wait," she said.

"He thinks I am a dream," Cerissa said sadly. "He is my mate if he will be with me. I would stay on land for him."

Mara reached in her purse for her cell phone. Unbelievably she had a signal. She found Mike's number and pressed call. He answered on the first ring. "Mara?"

"Say you have Facetime."

"I do, but—"

"Stop what you're doing and call me back right now." She used her bossiest teacher's voice.

He did, and his face appeared on her phone, frozen with concern.

"Here." She placed the phone in Cerissa's hands.

"Mike?" Cerissa sang his name in the odd musical way Mara was becoming accustomed to.

Mike's mouth fell open. "Sweetheart, I thought you were a dream."

"No dream," Cerissa trilled.

Desperate intensity replaced his shock. "Mara, where are you?"

She named the beach.

"I'll be there in five minutes. Don't move."

The connection cut out. "Mike?" Cerissa wailed as Mara pried the phone out of her hands.

Mara looked up and down the beach and spotted a towel caked with sand. She shook it out and draped it over Cerissa's shoulders, shielding her bare breasts.

"Pull your tail out of the water," Mara said. "In case people, humans, come."

Cerissa did, and her long, toned legs and wide, slightly webbed feet emerged. Mara rewrapped the towel around her, sarong style, just as what looked like a busload of people descended on the beach. Cerissa seemed nervous.

"It's okay," Mara said.

"Okay?" Cerissa asked.

Mike sprinted toward them, gasping for breath when he reached them.

Mara smiled. "Okay."

She left them there, oblivious to the rest of the world.

As she walked to her car, she fought off waves of nausea. Heeding a niggling voice in her head, she checked the date on her phone and noticed her monthly cycle should have started. Unaccountability nervous, she stopped at the drug store, grabbed a couple of boxes of tampons off the shelves, and wondered why the cashier looked at her so oddly when she paid.

Mara gathered her bag with a small smile and said thanks. Battling the urge to puke, she drove carefully along the winding road to her timeshare. Once inside, she pulled the boxes out of the bag and set them on the kitchen counter, willing herself to keep her lunch down.

She glanced at the boxes and gasped. One was a pregnancy test, the kind with instant results. She must have grabbed it by accident, when she picked up the tampons and hadn't noticed. No wonder it cost so much. Sweat beaded on her upper lip as she read the directions.

♥♥♥

Mara stared at the proof. She was pregnant.

Adrian had said it wasn't possible on land. But it was.

She was tempted to buy another one and take it again, but her continued nausea confirmed it. Wasn't this what she told Adrian she wanted in their chamber, before news of the quake reached Crystal City?

She stepped outside and walked in the sunshine, trying to commit the sight and scent of the bougainvillea and other flowers into her memory.

Focusing her thoughts, she silently called to Adrian, sending him her prayers of protection, a plea for him to return for her, and telling him that she carried his baby. She wandered back indoors and heard the ping of an email on her laptop. It was time to Skype with Gary.

She put the computer on her tiny kitchen table. She had an email from Kristen, full of her plans for the wedding she planned on Maui next summer. It ended with *Hope you're having hot monkey sex.*

Before she could draft an answer, Gary's face appeared on screen "Hey, bug."

"Hey," she said.

Jana appeared in the frame wearing her nurse's scrubs. She kissed Gary, waved to Mara, and smiled. "Your place looks amazing." She looked around the frame, did a double take, and said something to Gary that Mara couldn't hear. "I've got to go." She wouldn't meet Mara's gaze.

Mara stood up to get a drink of water and saw the pregnancy test box she'd left on the kitchen counter, right behind where she was sitting.

Crap.

"Mar?" Her brother's voice was strained with concern. "Sit." He used a tone she hadn't heard since she'd busted one of her mother's crystal goblets when she was eight or nine and he was left in charge.

Double crap.

She stretched her lips into a tight smile and then took a long sip of her water. It seemed to buoy up her resolve.

"You're pregnant," he said, as a statement of fact, without judgment, just concern.

"It seems I am," she said.

"How far along?" Her brother used his doctor voice, sounding clinical but kind.

She answered, in her matter of fact teacher voice, "Only just. I found out a minute before you emailed."

"How do you feel, bug?"

"Crazy hungry and nauseated," she said.

"Try to keep something in your stomach, like crackers," he said.

Mara nodded.

Gary raked his fingers through his hair, not a good sign. Crap. "So the father is a guy you met there or here?"

"Here," Mara said.

"You haven't told him yet, obviously, if you just found out."

"Obviously." She took a long sip of water and wondered why it felt like she was playing poker and bluffing her way with a losing hand.

"What is his name, Mar?"

"Adrian."

"Adrian what?" her brother growled. Now he was pissed.

"Adrian Lockhart." He had a lock on her heart, after

all, and every inch of her body. She felt color heat her cheeks.

"What does Adrian Lockhart do?"

In for a penny, in for a pound, she took a deep breath. "He's a marine geologist. He studies the ocean floor and deep sea environments. He goes all over the world, and I'm going with him."

Gary shook his head. "You, sweet sister, are lying your ass off."

Why did she think she could lie to him? He could always tell. She sighed. "You wouldn't believe me, Gar, if I told you who and what he really is. I barely believe it myself. But I love him."

"Try me," he said. "I work in the ER. There isn't much I haven't seen, or heard."

She spilled everything, Adrian, his sea form, and Crystal City.

"Has anyone else seen Adrian?" Gary asked, his face frozen with disbelief.

Mara fumed. He treated her as if she was one of her kindergartners. She said a rude word to piss him off then nodded. "And he asked me not to share because if anyone knew…" She trailed off, thinking of Mike and Cerissa, and clamped her mouth shut. She had no business exposing any more than she already had.

The moon was full tonight. She had gotten one text from Mike since Cerissa arrived, his message simple but clear. *Luv u kid, I owe U.*

"Call Mike tomorrow, or the next day, he's a reporter at the local newspaper here on the island. I had lunch with him that day when Mom was with you. You can verify my sanity with him."

He rubbed his forehead. "I've got to go. I have a shift."

"Is Jana good?" Mara's voice faltered. She'd come to love the petite ball of energy her brother had married.

Gary mumbled something then said a rude word. "Tomorrow, Mara, you and I will talk tomorrow. I think you've had an episode. I want you to go to a hospital."

"I love you," Mara choked out, knowing she wouldn't be going to any hospital. She had to leave.

"Don't do anything until I get there," he snapped, fear and love clouding his face. "For the love of God, Mara." He balled his hand into a fist.

She bit her lip to stem her impending tears and shut the computer off. She did a quick calculation. She wouldn't put it past her brother to board the next plane for Hawaii. So she had ten hours. She did the small bit of dirty laundry she had and packed her suitcase. She would donate the filled suitcase to charity. She could text Mike with the request.

She hand wrote Gary a long note, explaining how she never felt quite right in her own skin, how much she loved and trusted Adrian, and promising she would get word to him whenever she could. She told him how much she would miss him and Jana, how her heart broke to cause their mother more grief, but if she didn't go with Adrian, she may as well be dead.

She wrote an email to Kristen, explaining that she was having monkey sex with Adrian, a marine geologist she had fallen madly in love with who was doing research all over the world. She planned to travel the world with him, but would be back for Kristen's wedding on Maui next summer. She asked Kristen to tell the principal she quit and saved the email in the draft folder. She sealed the envelope and addressed it to Gary at the hospital so he could explain things to Jana when he felt the time was right. Mara would ask Mike to send the email to Kristen and mail the letter to Gary at the same time.

Done setting her life in order, she dressed in a wrap-around flowered sarong she'd purchased in a tourist shop, stuck a bloom of bougainvillea behind her ear, and walked to the beach.

The sun was setting and the full moon loomed in the midnight sky. Mara sat on the sand until dawn, her heart breaking while bitter tears rolled down her cheeks. She was pathetic, a crazy delusional bride waiting for no-show husband who wasn't even real.

She put her feet in the sea. Nothing happened. She was too afraid of the water to step in any farther. She wiggled her toes in the water, hoping for the tell-a-tale tingle. Nothing. Squaring her shoulders, she straightened, ripped the bloom from her hair, and cast it into the sea.

Gary was right. None of it made logical sense.

"I dreamed it all." She said it out loud. She would call Gary and tell him she had come to her senses. As for being pregnant? Maybe it was a false positive. She'd wait until she got home and have Gary run a new test.

When she stopped crying, she pulled the clothes out of her suitcase and put them back in the dresser. She fired up her laptop and answered Kristen's email, giving her opinion on wedding flowers and entrees for the wedding reception.

She would force herself to return to the islands next summer for her best friend's wedding. Thankfully it was on Maui and not here.

She had three weeks left on her timeshare and she would be damned if she would waste them being miserable. She would explore Fern Grotto today and take a scenic ride. But first, she needed a shower.

Chapter 10

Adrian had restored order to the reef somewhat when word came that Lorion had decreed that anything less than pristine restoration was unacceptable. If Adrian defied the old windbag, he risked a challenge to his right to rule when he got back to the Crystal City. It was a challenge he stood a good chance to lose since the cities beneath the riptides tightened habitat restoration standards by unanimous vote.

But if he didn't leave to get Mara before the fat moon waned, he would not be able to breach the deep currents to return to Crystal City with an inexperienced swimmer.

He ached for her—his Mara. The ache sliced deeper each moment they were apart. He swam to a dry place near the reef, what the humans called a cave, to clear his head. Light from vibrating crystals filled the space. He had the place to himself for a moment. It had been a few land days since he felt the sun or moon's energy above the water. Some sea forms didn't need or want to go above the waves to seek it, but he did. And Mara would miss it. He would have to ensure she got the doses of sun, moon, and starlight she needed.

He recalled the human myth of Hades and Persephone. Hades, the god of the underworld took his love, the goddess of springtime, to join with him in the underworld to the great sorrow of the goddess, her mother Demeter, who froze the land under ice until Hades allowed his love to live above the underworld for six land months. Nitia said the human legend had roots in the Turning Tides, when forms on land left for the sea to be dolphins, whales, and his people.

Even if it was possible for Mara to go back on land and live, Adrian knew he couldn't let her go away from him for half their existence. He stood on his land legs and paced the sanctuary, feeling the strong vibration of the crystals. He picked up a quartz shaped like a cylinder and pressed it to his forehead, above his nose to the spot the ancients called the third eye.

He saw Mara with the scribe taking food. His hand tightened painfully on the crystal, as if he could crush it into dust. He focused his attention on Mara. She wore the ruby necklace. He wished she would take off the colored circles that hid her eyes.

As if she heard his silent command, she slid them off. Her beautiful eyes were red and swollen, as if she'd been weeping. An icy current sliced through him. If that scribe had hurt her, he would end his life.

Then he heard Mara's words. She said that she had met somebody then said his name, "Adrian." She continued, telling the scribe they could only be friends.

Adrian hadn't realized he'd been holding his breath until he expelled it. He sat on a ledge and lowered the crystal, damning his laziness in his language classes. "Friend." He was almost certain friend was vastly different from twin flame or one you joined with.

He lifted the quartz again. This time Mara was alone outdoors, walking among the flowers. She lifted her face to the sunshine. Did she think she would never be on land again after she returned to Crystal City? There was so much to explain. His resolve hardened. He was done with Lorion's nonsense.

Adrian issued orders to Dracon, his second in command, and told him he was leaving.

Dracon chuckled.

Adrian shot him a stern, commanding look then laughed. He and Dracon had been what Mara called friends since before they were allowed to swim the seas alone.

"Safe journey, Dren."

Adrian smiled at Dracon's use of the shortened from of his given name.

"The old windbag won't guess you're not here," Dracon said.

"You will have honor for this, Drac," Adrian said.

Dracon used the hand motion for dismissal and chanted sounds for protection.

Adrian bowed his head in respect then set off.

ৎঙৎঙ

Mara checked her cell phone for messages. There were two missed calls, both from Gary. She called him back. Thankfully, he couldn't talk long because he was on duty.

"Hey, Gar."

"Mara—"

"No worries, bro." She cut him off. "We broke up. I'm not going anywhere other than home and back to work with my bitchy principal."

"Are you okay, bug?"

"I got my period," she said, hoping he couldn't tell she was lying.

Oh."

He asked her what she thought of stopping in San Francisco on her way back. "Jana and I could meet you."

"Sure." She tried to sound happy. "But what about Mom?"

He explained that Jana's sister would check in with her and they hung up.

She stripped and stepped into her shower. Some of her hair got caught in the necklace and she snapped the strands free, then she moved the stones around her neck, trying to find the clasp so she could take it off.

But she couldn't find it.

She wiped the steam off the bathroom mirror and examined it closely. She couldn't find an opening. She tried to break it apart with her hands, but it wouldn't budge. Fine, she'd stop at a jeweler on her way to Fern Grotto and get it taken off before it turned her neck green.

She smoothed sunscreen on her face, neck, arms, and legs and fastened her hair in a ponytail to make it easier for the jeweler to cut the necklace off. She didn't bother with makeup.

❧❧❧

The elderly gentleman in the elegant jewelry store excused himself from the couple he was waiting on and hurried to where Mara stood looking at gold charms in the display case.

Her eyes immediately found a mermaid with a beautiful filigree tail.

Perfect.

She shook her head in disgust. She would have to make an appointment to see a psychiatrist and gynecologist soon.

The man peered at her necklace through eyeglasses perched on the end of his nose then pulled out a jeweler's glass. "May I, miss?" He gestured to her necklace.

Mara leaned toward him to give him a better look. "I can't find the clasp and want to take it off. Could you cut it?"

The jeweler gasped. "Miss, come with me."

She followed him to a backroom. She could hear the other couple talking, so she figured she was safe.

"These jewels, these rubies, miss, are such that I have never seen in my thirty years of appraising gems. And the gold is more than twenty-four karat. It's worth a small fortune. I see no clasp to remove this."

Mara struggled to speak through the knot in her throat. "Are you saying this is real?"

He nodded, touching the stones with reverence. "Priceless, miss." He reached for her hand. "I fear for you. If someone realizes this value, they could harm you to get it. "

"Cut it off then," Mara said.

The jeweler shook his head. "I could try, but the tensile strength—may I photograph it to document it?"

She nodded.

"Think about this, at least for a day, then if you come back, we'll try to remove it, if that's what you want. Conceal this under your clothing and do not speak of the value."

Mara was breathing hard. A wave of nausea hit her hard. How could this be real? "How much is the mermaid charm?" She spoke in a voice barely above a whisper.

"Ahh." The jeweler kept hold of her hand as they walked toward the case. He held one finger up to the couple. "I'll be right with you."

He extracted the mermaid and slipped the charm onto a thin filigree gold bracelet and fastened it on her arm.

"How much?" she asked, although she knew she'd likely have to max out her credit card to pay for it.

"No charge, beautiful child," he said. "You were chosen. I see that now."

"I couldn't," she said.

"Please," the jeweler said,

"All right." Mara stumbled back to her car.

Chapter 11

The typhoon was unexpected. Adrian was forced to take refuge in Crystal City.

"She wants the necklace removed." Lorion set down the quartz crystal he'd held to his forehead. "She also feels sick in her stomach at the thought of joining with you."

"No," Adrian exploded, disgusted that the old windbag witnessed his frustration.

"My son is ready to assume his duties, or you can take a second wife from a city in the alliance to satisfy the terms of the treaty," Lorion said. "Time is up."

Nitia touched Adrian lightly on his shoulder. "I too

look through the crystals," she said. "Mara has joined with you."

"I know," Adrian said.

"I mean she has a baby," she said

"It is not possible," Lorion blustered, his face purple with rage.

Adrian drew Nitia to a private chamber. He ran his fingers through his hair.

"You are partly human," Nitia said. "You joined on land?"

"Yes," Adrian said.

"She made preparations and waited on the sand the night of the fat moon," his aunt continued.

"And I didn't come." He clenched his jaw.

"One of our kind went on land that night. Mara helped her to be with the scribe. She is still there."

Adrian knew he could give up his right to rule the Crystal City, but he could not give up Mara, ever. He would bridge time and space to be with her. Sea forms of his rank could do this three times in their existence. He'd done it once before to be with Mara in her sleeping state. He could do so now. It would leave him with one more time. Maybe he could use it to circumvent the typhoon and bring Mara back to Crystal City.

"I will go back to her," Adrian said.

His aunt followed him to the sacred chamber filled with minerals the humans deemed precious.

He did not want to look in the crystals when he could

do nothing to soothe Mara's distress. He did so then and saw that she was still on the island.

Nitia touched her cheek to Adrian's and chanted words of protection.

ფოფ

Mike texted Mara saying he was taking a few days off work. She didn't want to intrude on his and Cerissa's time together, but she really wanted to pump Cerissa for answers. "Lunch?" she texted, not expecting an answer.

His answer was immediate. *Zeke's? noon okay?*

Cool. She was crazy hungry.

Mike was protective and sweetly possessive of Cerissa, who received her share of hungry male stares as Mike led her to the table. The trio sat outdoors on a covered patio.

Cerissa giggled when she saw Mara. "Adrian is coming," she said.

"What?" Mara said it so loud she drew stares. Nausea and nerves seized her. She lowered her voice. She was one hot mess.

The same waitress from before came then, looking concerned. "You okay?"

Mara nodded. "I'll have crab cakes and chocolate cake with ice tea."

"Sure, baby." The waitress's concern triggered a fresh round of tears.

Oblivious to Mara's turmoil, Cerissa ordered shrimp. Mike ordered mahi mahi, but changed to shrimp when he saw the look on Cerissa's face.

"Cerissa, how do you know Adrian is coming?" Mara said.

Cerissa nuzzled Mike's neck and shrugged.

"She's still learning English," Mike said.

Mara offered a shaky smile, tried her kindergartner teacher's approach, and used a prop. She pulled out her ruby necklace. "Do you know about this?" She pointed to the necklace.

"All sea forms know," Cerissa said.

"What does it mean?" Mara asked.

Mike rubbed Cerissa's well-toned shoulders, bare in a tank top. "You are Adrian's for always," she said, not really answering Mara's question.

When their food came, Mara couldn't put it in her stomach fast enough. When the daily rain shower came Cerissa laughed in joy and drew deep breaths. Even Mara found a small pool of calmness in the smell of the pure water.

"She loves to smell the rain, but she has to stay dry, you know?" Mike murmured.

"I think I'm losing my mind," Mara said.

"Sweetheart, no." He reached across the table and squeezed her hand, keeping his other arm firmly around Cerissa's shoulders.

"My brother's about to have me committed." Mara

ate the last bite of crab cakes. "You're a journalist, you report facts. How does this make logical sense?"

"It doesn't. All I know is that she's here in my arms, and I want to keep her forever. I don't know if it's possible, but Cerissa talks as if—if she's here, you can be there." He kissed Cerissa's head.

Cerissa moved closer to him until she was nearly in his lap. She beamed at Mara. "You stay with Adrian in Crystal City. You rule with him."

Cerissa's eyes wandered to the wooden carving of the mermaid that hung over the bar. She scrambled away from Mike and out of the booth, to dart through tables to the bar. Mike sat, but kept a steady eye on Cerissa.

Mara searched her heart and came to an unbelievable, but necessary choice. "Mike, there's a letter in the timeshare addressed to my brother and an email in the draft folder to my friend Kristen. Mail the letter and send the email, please? If what she said is true."

"Sure." He slid out of the booth as a man in surfer gear sidled up to Cerissa.

"I should go," Mara said to herself. She fished some money out of her purse and left her share of the bill on the table.

Cerissa caught up to her in the parking lot. She grasped Mara's arm. "You must join Adrian soon. Must be Mara's free will."

Mike ran up behind Cerissa and took hold of her waist. The mermaid sighed and melted against him. Trying to ignore the ache in her chest, Mara left them and went back to her timeshare.

She put on the scraps of bikini Kristen had convinced her to buy, picked up the quartz crystal she kept on her bedside, then took a mat to the beach. She laid in the sand, the quartz resting on her forehead above the bridge of her nose, as the moon inched higher into the inky black sky dotted with a million stars. Images cascaded in her mind. Adrian arguing with Lorion. Adrian pacing alone in a chamber filled with light, saying her name. Adrian in his sea form hurtling toward a vortex of water.

Shaking, Mara dropped the crystal on the mat and waded into the shallows. She didn't feel the tingling that signaled her own sea form, only the tug of the waves, ushering her out farther. Although engulfed with panic, she forced her feet to stumble deeper into the waves.

Longing for Adrian seized her like a riptide that threatened to drown her. She fingered the ruby necklace, by which he had staked his claim to her, and centered her thoughts. "I am waiting," she called above the waves. "I love you, Adrian," she shouted. "Forever, it is done."

The tide curled around her, slowly dragging her farther out. She didn't fight, letting the riptide pull her down—down to dark waters. She couldn't see her hand in front of her face. She gripped the ruby necklace. She needed to pull air into her lungs, but she knew she'd never make it to the surface.

She stilled in the water and felt her feet tingle. She

untied her bathing suit bottom, freeing it seconds before she took full sea form. She rode the riptide, hoping those in Crystal City would find her body and save her unborn baby.

The screaming need for air had her gasping. The sea poured into her lungs. Her last thought was of Adrian and the gold lights of mischief in his eyes as she succumbed. Vaguely she felt something clamp hard around her waist, then she was nothing but essence of the pure water.

Chapter 12

Caught in the riptide, Adrian clamped his mouth onto Mara's. She wasn't moving. He ripped off the material covering her breasts and pinched her nipples hard, as he blasted air into her lungs. The orange and blue hues of her tail were fading. Desperation had him fusing his mouth to hers, forcing his life force into her. It would leave him weak, but he didn't care. He would rest before they journeyed back to Crystal City. And they would return together.

She moved in his arms, then her hands touched his shoulders. She grabbed onto his hair and sagged against him. He kissed her, their tongues intertwining as he gave her the oxygen she needed. He swam fast for the surface, keeping a firm hold of Mara, hoping they were near dry land.

He broke surface and scanned the horizon. The sun was high in the sky. Mara, starved for oxygen, panted in his arms. She tried to speak but he stopped her. "No, darling. Not yet. You must gain life force."

He spotted a speck of sand and a tree, and hauled Mara toward it. He pushed her through the shallows then sat on the sand, scanning the island for signs of humans. There were none, just the lone tree holding coconuts.

When they lost their sea forms, he pulled Mara to her feet then lifted her into his arms to explore the island.

"Adrian?"

"No," he said. "I am not allowing you to speak yet." He fused his mouth to her neck, knowing he would mark her skin. She sighed and melted against him.

He found a structure built by humans, long left abandoned. He swept through the cobwebs spanning the doorway and set Mara on a table. Bright spots of color dotted her cheeks. He moved between her legs and kissed her fiercely.

She put her hands in his long hair and pulled hard. He lifted his mouth and arched an eyebrow at her. She opened her mouth then licked her lips nervously. He touched his forehead to hers and tugged on her necklace, inhaling her scent that reminded him of wild roses.

How could he have left her?

જ્જ

Mara brushed her cheek against the hand that held the necklace. "I'm okay now," she whispered. "I promise."

Adrian looked at her doubtfully.

"I think the soldiers used this place during World War II. My dad watched the Military Channel a lot." Catching his puzzled expression, she explained, "On TV, television."

Mischief lit his eyes. "Like *Survivor*?"

She gasped. "You watch television in Crystal City?"

He shrugged. "At times."

Together they wandered around the hut, not that there was much to see. A table and single cot made of wood and canvas covered with a brown scratchy Army blanket made up the furnishings. Mara picked up a dusty package of cobweb encrusted K-rations on a nearby shelf, disturbing a hidden yellow snake. She shrieked and dropped the K-ration package as the snake slithered away. With an incomprehensible word, Adrian pulled her behind him and chuckled. The snake slid out of the hut.

She grabbed Adrian by the shoulders and tried not to be distracted by his smooth, toned chest. "Snakes can be poisonous to humans, Adrian."

Puzzlement erased his humor.

"Snakes bite, kill people, make them dead, stop breathing," she explained.

He shook his head, drew her against him until she rested under his chin. His erection pressed into her. "Mara never stop breathing, ever again."

She could stay in his arms forever, but she had to make him understand. She cupped his face and tugged it down to hers. "Darling, some snakes…" She raised one hand and imitated the snake's movement. "…hurt humans."

He caught her hand and laughed. "No, Mara. You take sea form." He mimicked her movement with his hand and repeated the unintelligible word from before. "Not hurt you."

"Oh." She left his arms and picked up the K-ration package. She grinned and shuddered at the thought of eating seventy-year-old K-rations. "Now this would kill both of us."

His gaze dipped between the package she held and her grin. "We must stay here before we return to Crystal City, seven times the earth turns. We eat fish. I show you how." He cocked his head. "Like *Survivor*."

"There's coconuts, too. Like *Gilligan's Island*, on TV." A sharp ache twisted her stomach. Hunger or something worse? It hit her then, Adrian didn't know about the baby. Had it survived?

She thumped down hard on the cot, raising a cloud of dust. Her hand covered her naked stomach.

His eyes grew wide with alarm. He rushed to her side and took her chin in his hand, forcing her to look at him.

Tears rolled down her face. What if she had harmed their baby while she tried to convince herself he was a figment of her imagination? She swallowed hard.

Adrian's eyes darkened with concern. "Mara?"

Guilt flooded her and she dropped her gaze. "I'm pregnant."

"What is pregnant?" His question was gentle as he lifted her face and wiped her tears with his thumb.

"Baby." She put his hand on her slender stomach. "Our baby, inside me."

His face went blank. "You not want babies." His voice was flat, not asking but stating a fact.

"No." Flustered, she tangled her fingers in his hair and gave a short tug. "I mean, yes. I want your babies."

He fused his mouth to hers, his tongue dueling with hers. He broke off the kiss, raising his head until their lips barely touched as he breathed the air she exhaled.

"I'm afraid I may have hurt the baby when I went into the water and stopped breathing," she said.

His smile was tender and the love in his eyes made her toes curl. "Nitia saw in the crystals that you had our baby." He pressed his lips to hers in a soft kiss. "When I found you, I gave you my life force so you have air. I felt baby inside you then."

Joy rose, and she gave a delighted squeal.

Adrian took hold of her chin again. "We get food. Unless you eat snake?" he teased.

She shuddered at the thought. "No."

He took her hand and led her outside to the tree where a couple of coconuts had fallen.

"How will we open them?" she asked.

He reached down and picked one up. He pointed out the ridges at the end of the coconut, and then demonstrated his answer by thwacking it against a large rock, cracking it in two pieces.

"Oh," she said.

He dribbled the coconut milk into her mouth before he drank. When they'd drunk their fill, he pulled a seashell from the water and scraped the white pulp, feeding it to her first. He left the empty coconut shells on the sand then moved toward the water. She followed him, but he said a word in his language. "Wait." He pointed to where she'd left the coconuts.

"No." She held onto his waist. "Don't leave me, never again."

His gaze raked over her naked body and heated with need. He tugged on her necklace until she was pressed into his length.

"Mine, Mara." He pressed his lips to hers and she opened. Her tongue dueled with his, until he groaned and moved them onto the sand under the coconut tree. She forced him to lie back so she could straddle him. He grinned.

She drew him to her sex and slid down his thick erection, moaning as he stretched and filled her. "Mine, Adrian," she whispered.

He tugged her necklace, bringing her face to his and fusing his mouth to hers. She broke the kiss and rode him hard. He rubbed her sex until she came, screaming his name. He circled his hips, hitting her G-spot until she came again as he reached his climax, emptying himself inside her. He rolled her to his side and tucked her under his chin.

"Damn," she said.

"What is damn?" His mouth nibbled her ear.

"This, us, how we join," she said.

He laughed. "Damn."

The rest of the afternoon passed as he showed her how to harvest the small fish in the shallows for sustenance. He explained it would take time in her sea form for her eyes to see in the murkier depths of the ocean where other, bigger fish lived. She insisted on cleaning the tiny fish with the sharp seashells he found. Then she poked the tiny bits on sticks and roasted them over a fire she made with wooden matches unearthed in the hut and dried out leaves from the lone tree. Her smoky fire seemed to make him nervous, and he ate his catch raw. Since she didn't have the strength, she let him crack the coconuts open.

She felt restless and in need of a change of scene so she asked him if they could walk on the beach. Instead, they swam in the ocean. Adrian kept giving her possessive and hungry looks as she flashed her brilliant tail. She was amazed at how comfortable she felt with her nakedness. Of course, her attention kept drifting to his golden, olive skin and toned muscles. His thick, wavy hair was held back from his face by a narrow band of palm leaf, but it didn't detract from his masculine beauty.

Later as the stars began to dot the sky, Adrian decided to teach her the words in his language for parts of her body. He settled her between his legs on the sand and tried to start the lesson, but he ended up teasing and sucking her nipples.

He continued to her sex until she begged him to plunge inside her. She lost count of how many times he'd brought her to a screaming climax.

During the long, sunny days she told him about her childhood in Michigan, while he shared his life in Crystal City. They had to be back in the Crystal City in four days so Adrian could claim his right to rule, but he was in no hurry to start the journey, which puzzled her. He explained how hundreds of thousands of years ago his distant ancestors had lived on land before migrating to the sea. When she pressed for more, he told her she would have a chance to learn more once they returned to Crystal City.

"Was it hard being half human?" She regretted her question when his body stiffened.

He said words in his language and then answered her in English. "At times. I am of the ruling line so it was…" He paused, searching for words. "…bad not."

"Not bad," Mara corrected, her experience teaching

children to speak English kicking in. "In English we say 'not bad.'"

"Hmm." He nuzzled her neck, sending a jolt of desire racing to her core. "This is also not bad." He inserted his fingers into her sex and found evidence of her arousal.

All her questions vanished as he rolled her under him and took her again and again, spilling his seed inside her only after she screamed his name with each release.

It wasn't until their third day on the island, as she roasted bits of fish over the smoky fire, that she remembered something she wanted to ask him. When he crouched down beside her, she swallowed hard. "The baby," she began then stopped.

He smiled.

Gathering her courage, she plowed forward. "If it was born on land, if you had been born on land..." She couldn't figure how to end that thought.

His smile faded and he traced circles on her breasts. "Babies learn sea form same as how to walk on legs."

"So if you weren't in the sea?" she prompted, even as the thought of leaving her family and friends had tears welling.

What would she do in the Crystal City? On land she could barely keep a job, but she loved to teach. She had nothing to offer Adrian's civilization. She would be useless. Maybe she needed more time to sort things out. And what about her mother? What kind of horrible person abandoned their mother?

"You are sad to leave land." He lifted her chin forcing her to look at him. All she could do was nod. "Baby would not learn sea form unless he was in sea for teaching."

"He? It's a boy?"

Adrian nodded, kissed her gently, and then left her to walk to the hut.

☙❧

Frustration welled in Adrian. He was asking more of her than she could give. He surveyed the hut in an effort to get himself under control and resist the urge to take hold of Mara and return to Crystal City that very moment, bending time and space to do it. But she must come to him of her own free will.

Her smoky fires could have alerted other humans that people were marooned on this uninhabited island. It wouldn't be long before humans came to rescue them.

If she wouldn't leave the land, he could stay with her until the other humans came to help. Her brother had undoubtedly raised an alarm by now since she had not contacted him. Once she was safe with the humans, her own kind, he would return to Crystal City alone.

Bitter bile rose in his throat. Mara was his. They were twin flames.

Stepping out of the hut, he stared at the cloudless sky. He was strong enough now to make the journey back to Crystal City with her and arrive in time to assume the mantle of leadership. If she chose to stay behind, she would not be safe on the island alone. Did she love him enough to leave everything and everyone she knew and loved to come with him?

♥♥

Mara heard the low thrum of the seaplane engine before she could see it. She screamed for Adrian and he was instantly there, anchoring her to his side.

"I must leave for deepest ocean now, Mara." He looked into her eyes and smiled sadly. "You go back."

"We could go with the pilot so I could say goodbye to Gary," she pleaded.

"No, Mara. I leave now." He touched his forehead to hers. His eyes, faded to murky hazel, shimmered with tears. "You wish to stay on land." He didn't wait for her answer, but turned toward the sea, leaving her on the beach.

Watching him leave, she thought of her loved ones. Gary who would likely worry sick over her. Sweet Kristen, the dear Bridezilla who buoyed her up when she could do nothing right for their bitchy principal. Her mother, who had given her sweet blessing, even though Mara would never see her again. And Adrian, who made her real.

The plane came closer.

"Adrian!" She splashed into the shallows. "I am ready."

He turned. "Are you certain, darling?"

Mara drank in the sight of the male she had joined with, his auburn hair, gold skin, and tight toned torso. Her gaze traced over the clean lines of his handsome face and his full lips which were curved into a smile. She recalled every time he kissed her, how it made her feel alive. How desire roared between them with every touch.

She flew into his arms. "I can't live unless you're near me. I was half dead before you found me in my dreams. I never felt right in my body. I lived only for my dreams when you were inside me. I love you, your sea form, and mine too." She lowered her eyes. "I will make mistakes in the Crystal City."

He took hold of her and kissed her. When he lifted his lips, he sang words in the language of the sea. The melody calmed the stormy waves in the deepest recesses of her soul, even as the engine of the seaplane came closer.

"The ones you love on land," Adrian said, looking deep into her eyes.

She touched his beautiful mouth with her fingertips. "We'll find a way, darling, between the two of us we'll figure it out."

He raised an eyebrow.

She touched the top of his head. "We'll use our brains to solve the problem. Intelligently."

He tugged her ruby necklace then palmed her breasts. "You, also, Mara mine."

She shivered at the possessive gleam in his eyes. "Adrian?" She bit her lip as he took firm hold of her waist to pull her into deeper water.

"Yes, darling?" he said.

"I will be your only wife?"

His eyes lit with gold. "Yes, and I will be the only one you join with. Nobody else will have you."

She smiled and melted against him. "Thank God."

They could see the plane overhead.

"It is time," Adrian said.

She smiled into his eyes, entrusting him with her body, her heart, and her soul. "Forever, it is done," she whispered before his mouth fused to hers, stealing away her human breath. She caressed his erection as the now familiar tingling in her feet spread to her waist. Her glorious sea form unfurled in vivid orange and blue. Held safe in Adrian's arms, she began her journey to their home.

THE END

About the Author

Tara Eldana is an award-winning staff writer for a weekly community newspaper chain in metro Detroit. She became hooked on romance fiction when her eleventh grade English teacher rejected the book report she wrote, saying the book was much too easy for her, and insisted she read and report on Daphne du Maurier's *Rebecca*. Eldana had read Margaret Mitchell's *Gone With the Wind* that previous summer.

Eldana took a long road through J-school, graduating from Oakland University in Rochester, Michigan in '95, just shy of 20 years after she finished high school, raising a couple kids, working part-time, and doing her homework while her husband and kids watched TV. Still she found time to read what her kids called her "mush books."

She loves the romance genre and loves letting her characters take control of their stories. Eldana is a member of the Greater Detroit Romance Writers of America.

www.ingramcontent.com/pod-product-compliance
Lightning Source LLC
Chambersburg PA
CBHW071003120726
47910CB00004B/1367